Black Ink Publications Presents

BAD COP

A Novel By

Sa'id Salaam

Email: saidmsalaam@gmail.com and/or
blackinkpublications1@gmail.com
Facebook: Free Sa'id Salaam
Cover design and layout by: Sunny Giovanni
Edited by:

Acknowledgments

Bismillah Ir Rahman Ir Raheem
As always, First and Foremost All praise and worship is
for Almighty God, alone, with no partners. I bear witness that
there is nothing worthy of worship except Him.

BAD COP

A Novel By

Sa'id Salaam

Prologue

I hate funerals. Any funeral but especially cop funerals, they are the worse. A bunch of phony mother fuckers rejoicing that it was you instead of them laying in that box. Then, what's up with the kilts and bag pipes? Like all cops are Irish or some shit. Then your so-called brothers all misty eyed even though racism is alive and kicking in the force. Department preacher singing your praises no matter if you were straight as an arrow or crooked as a fish hook. Most of these guys and gals need to be in jail themselves. That vice detective in the front row got the biggest child porn collection in the Tristate area. The lady cop next to him sell more pussy than the law allows. The so-called drug taskforce got more dope in the street than the cartel but, who am I to talk huh? Just look at the position I got myself into. Laid out with my academy picture beside a closed casket. You know it's ugly when they have to close the lid on you.

Yeah, I hate funerals, especially cop funerals, especially when it's mine.

Chapter 1

I came along way from a happy, chubby girl growing up in a big house on Long Island to a dead cop in Atlanta. Most New Yorkers move south to slow down, prosper and live. Not me, nope. I came down here, got in a whole bunch of trouble and got my ass killed. It's a long story so let's start from the beginning.

"How's my, baby!" Officer Rohan Robinson sang as he came out of the bedroom dressed in his uniform. His East Indian heritage gave his skin a nice golden tone while his hair was almost straight. His dark-skinned wife, Michelle, knew the combination would make some pretty children and more importantly give them good hair.

She envisioned a bunch of handsome, curly-headed boys, but all she got was one daughter. A pretty, little girl who would never need a perm, but boys are not the same as girls. She'd come from a household of five boys with her being the lone girl. She'd seen how differently her parents treated her from them. She went from wanting to be a boy to wanting nothing but boys.

"Hey, baby, I..." Michelle began but Rohan wasn't talking to her and scooped up their daughter Megan instead.

"Hey, Daddy!" the little girl squealed in delight as he blew raspberries on her chubby cheeks. The happy child's skin tone was exactly like her dad's and she had big, black, bouncy curls for hair. Being an only child and spoiled by her father made her a fat but happy child. Michelle wore a jealous scowl at playing second fiddle but quickly erased it when Rohan turned her way.

"And my darling wife?" he greeted extending his arm so she could join the group hug.

They had just quietly made love before he showered and dressed for his night shift. Their theme song, *Just in Case I Don't Make It Home Tonight,* had played in the background to ensure that their child didn't hear the moans and groans of her pursuit of another child. He could get some more when he got home since their daughter would be off to school.

"Last, but not least," she quipped as she joined the embrace. Megan reached to squeeze her neck as well. The gifted 7-year-old was smart enough to notice the temperature change whenever her father left. What she couldn't add, subtract or multiply but saw was her mother's jealousy over her. She was too young to understand what it was but sure felt it.

"You know I love my ladies, don't you?" he asked needlessly. He proved his love and devotion to his family on a regular basis.

He'd secured them a big house out on Long Island that seemed to be a million miles away from the south Bronx projects they'd come from. Two brand new cars set in the driveway and clothes filled the closet. Rohan had made it his mission in life to protect and serve, and it started at home with his family first. Being overextended forced him to work several double shifts each week.

"Yes!" they sang in chorus and squeezed him again. He closed his eyes and basked in the love before heading out into the dangerous streets of Harlem.

"Love you guys. See you in the morning," he proclaimed and gave each a parting kiss. Michelle blushed knowing just how he would see her when he got in. Both smiled and waved as he exited the house and entered his car. They kept smiling and waving until he was out of sight.

"Wanna watch a movie with me?" Megan turned and asked hopefully before the temperature dropped.

"Nah," Michelle said turning up the corner of her lip. It really wasn't the child's fault that she reminded her of the stuck up pretty girls who'd taunted her about her dark skin and course hair, and it definitely wasn't her fault that she'd given birth to her and not the brood of sons she longed for. She just couldn't seem to get pregnant again, even though they had sex daily.

Mother and daughter went their separate ways to do their separate thing. For the girl that meant the daunting task of trying to figure out which toys to play with. She had Barbie this and Barbie that, not to mention every video game system available in those days. The smart child's number one past time was the encyclopedia set. Just something else for her ratchet mother to talk about.

Michelle went and got on the phone with her friend Reese back in the Bronx. The two had grown up together in the same projects. They'd smoked the same weed, worn the same clothes and slept with the same dudes. Michelle, however, happen to catch Rohan's eye in a club and the rest was history. She would have slept with him that first night, but he had school the next day. He was so busy they didn't get a chance to hang out for a couple of weeks. Once the nerd from Queens got a taste of the hoe from the Bronx he was hooked. He proposed weeks later.

Reese, on the other hand, was still doing the same thing resulting in four baby daddies and a case of genital warts. They didn't get to hang out much but spoke almost daily. Michelle loved to brag about her husband, house, car and life. Reese always congratulated her but secretly despised her.

"So, Rohan just upgraded my truck. You know, you need an SUV out here in the suburbs. You're so lucky to still be in the projects. Bus stop right out in front and you can always catch a gypsy cab," Michelle bragged and dissed at the same time. Two fucked up people can never really be friends but they can relate.

"Mmhm," Reese hummed since she was holding in smoke from the blunt she was smoking. She'd laced it with powdered cocaine to make the high, higher and last longer. Some call it a 'woolie' or 'dirty' but it should be called 'strike one' on the way to striking out. Most crack heads start off light like this. Then, get a stripe and graduate to the pipe, aka strike three.

"So, what you been up to girl?" she asked knowing it wasn't shit to be up to in the projects. Old folks still lived there because it was all they could afford. They just waited on their reservation to the upper room. The young ones with vision escaped and never came back. The others sold drugs and made babies, while also waiting to die.

"Just chilling. My babies' daddies coming through with that check, so I been straight. Hitting the club err night," she relayed between tokes.

Michelle could hear her smoking and wished she could get a pull. Just one long toke, and a line. Just one long, thick line of coke. Oh, and a big swig from a 40 like back in the days. She twisted her lips ruefully, knowing that wasn't going to happen. Not with a cop for a husband. Not just a cop, but one of Manhattan's best narcotic cops.

Meanwhile, Megan read two books at the same time. One was for school and the other just because she loved to read. Books were like an all-expense paid vacation to wherever. She'd already visited 15 countries on 3 different continents. Her actions and adventures were nothing compared to what her father had going on.

Chapter 2

"Sup 'potna. You love that monkey suit, I see!" Rohan's much younger partner Jackson greeted as he entered the locker room. The light-skinned, pretty boy dressed like the rapper/rock star he envisioned himself as.

"My daughter loves my uniform," he replied as he began to change out of it. It was partially true since Megan did love to see her hero in uniform, but he also loved wearing it just as much. He was proud to be a New York City police officer. Even after his promotion to detective and plain clothes he still wore his blues every chance he got.

"I need to swing through and see my kid," he said like he only had one. He made almost as many babies as he did arrest but only counted the one by his main chick. A hot-blooded Puerto Rican with a hot head and even hotter vagina. Their tumultuous relationship revolved around fighting, fucking and shopping.

"Yeah," Rohan grunted and bit his tongue. He couldn't imagine not seeing his beautiful daughter every day. That's why he worked so hard to make sure he came home every night. Just another example of how incompatible he and Jackson were.

Jax was a cowboy. A rooting, tooting, two gun shooting cowboy.

They were in the middle of a big undercover operation that would get them both either promoted or dead. A win/win since either way since once it was over he wouldn't have to work with the man anymore. He may have not seen the man take money but it was obvious that he did. Unfortunately, amongst his coworkers it was the rule and not the exception. Why should the dope boys have all the fun with all the money, cars and women?

"So, Snake wants to meet us at Back Shots!" Jax cheered rubbing his hands together like dinner was being served. Back Shots was a high-end strip club known for having the baddest bad girls in the city.

"Why not City Island or Lobster and Crabs?" Rohan wanted to know. He was a married man and hated being around a bunch of women; especially some of the baddest bad girls in the city completely naked. He could see himself speeding home in the morning to rush inside of his wife for relief. Michelle would of course complain about him smelling like baby oil with glitter on his face.

"Or...Back Shots, home of big titties, fat asses, blow jobs and shit. Bet Michelle gives you killer blow jobs," he cheered.

"Jax, you obviously can't see it, but there's a line, and you crossed it," Rohan calmly explained. He knew his partner well enough to know most of his words came straight out his mouth without ever passing through his brain. A normal person's brain will filter inappropriate shit and allow a person to keep it to themselves.

"My bad! I know you married guys are sensitive. Tender dicks, nothing wrong with that," he offered. It was probably as close as he would get to an actual apology so Rohan let it be.

"No problem. You ready?" he asked after transforming into his street clothes and persona. He went by the name Tonto, a moniker his Indian looks got him called as a child coming up. Tonto was the wrong kind of Indian, but he embraced it anyway. He looked every bit the part in a tailored suite and chunky platinum jewelry.

Jax on the other hand lived the part 24/7. He didn't have to change clothes because he dressed like a dope boy every day. Complete with an easy hundred grand worth of jewels dripping from his neck, ears, fingers and wrist. He pushed a spanking new STS Caddie and had a Porsche parked at his Brooklyn condo.

"Gotta take a quick shit," he said holding up a finger. He did that quite often making his partner assume he had a digestive problem. He had a problem alright but it wasn't IBS.

Jax rushed into a stall and shimmied out of his skinny pants and silk drawers. He sat his bare ass cheeks down on the toilet and dug into his pocket. His pretty smile spread across his handsome face when he saw the glistening cocaine in a hundred-dollar bill. That smile turned into a grimace as he took a heaping scoop up each nostril.

"Argh! This shit is the shit!" he congratulated. He knew he'd come up on some fish scale when they busted a dealer in Washington Heights. The coke was so pretty he'd grabbed a few handfuls to keep for himself. That and twenty grand from the pile of money.

"Straight now?" Rohan asked when he returned. He noticed an extra ping and zip in the man but knew a good shit can do that so paid it no mind.

"Super straight," he shot back, super high. He followed his partner out of the precinct into the parking lot. A press of a key fob made a Lexus beep in response. "Piece of shit they got us riding in."

"The Lexus?" Rohan shot back in shock. He knew full well it started at ninety grand because Michelle had just tried to talk him into buying one. Jax was right, she did have some killer head, she'd used it that morning to help her campaign. In the end, she had to settle on a new truck that was close to sixty-grand instead.

"Jap crap! You gotta drive the new Porsche!" he shot back and climbed behind the wheel.

"Still, be easy," he recommended since he drove like a bat out of hell. The last thing they needed was to get pulled over by other cops, which could blow their cover.

"I got this," he assured him as he eased out of the parking lot. As soon as he hit the street he mashed the gas and drove like a bat out of hell out to the Bronx.

****

"They just called. Said they on the way," XL announced to his boss. Despite being 6'5" and three-hundred-pounds he pulled double duty as secretary along with his role as body guard.

"Shit, we get us a good Queens dealer and that's the whole city!" Snake cheered. His Columbian connect was dumping as much work on him as he could handle. He fancied himself the Amazon of cocaine, distributing it all over the city. He was mulling over the idea of using drones to deliver to the five boroughs. A few table dances later Jax and Tonto entered the club.

"That's what the fuck I'm talking about!" Jax said and literally clapped his hands at the wall to wall strippers. The club boasted almost every ethnic group on the planet. They even had an Eskimo shaking her flat ass on a side stage.

"Let's handle our business, and get up out of here," Rohan said, seeing the same tits and asses but with the opposite effect. He wanted to get far away while his partner wanted to get deep inside.

"Bruh, don't be a tight ass. Don't act like a fucking cop!" Jax warned through clenched teeth. Being undercover meant becoming a criminal. Jax embraced it wholeheartedly while it was the part Rohan struggled with.

"There they are," he said, seeing XL stand in the VIP section and raise his large hand. He hit an internal switch and became Tonto. Jax, however, never had to turn on or off for that matter since he was always on.

Jax smiled and groped his way through a swamp of naked women. Rohan just knew their perfumes were rubbing off on him. Michelle would certainly have something to say about that. The bouncer charged with keeping the common folk from the VIP parted the velvet rope.

"Jax! Tonto!" Snake stood and greeted warmly when they reached his table. XL stood back with a menacing scowl on his face like a good bodyguard does. Luckily, the phone didn't ring and expose his secretarial side.

"Sup yo!" Jax greeted with a pound and man hug. Tonto stepped up next and did the same.

"Ready to handle some business?" Tonto asked as soon as they sat. He almost got kicked under the table by his partner for moving so fast.

"In a minute. Let's have a drink. Watch some asses shake," Snake said being a good host. He raised his hand and the waitress made a beeline to their table.

"What can I get you, baby?" the woman, who looked like she could be on one of the stages herself, asked. Her tiny shorts were pulled up into her crotch to show it off while a set of heavy breasts gave her wife beater all it could handle. Big nipples strained against the fabric like a nosey set of eyes trying to get a peek.

"Henny. Bring the bottle," he suggested and she took off to fill the order.

"Bruh, I would bend her over the table and eat her from the back!" Jax vowed.

"You want to? You can," Snake offered, raising his eyebrows. Jax opened his mouth to shout a 'hell yeah' but was interrupted by the DJ.

"Now coming to center stage...the one...the only...Pocahontas!" he said, throwing the record on.

A voluptuous brown-skinned woman with jet black hair took the stage dressed in full Cherokee regalia. Tonto squinted past the feathers and war paint. Overlooking the big brown breast with large darker brown nipples he saw his little sister Maria. He felt the urge to rush the stage and drag her home to their mother, just like he'd done most of their life. His baby sister was addicted to the streets, therefore there was no saving her until she wanted to be saved.

"That's your type ain't it, bruh?" Jax asked excitedly when he saw his partner's gaze stuck on the stripper on the stage. Usually the man lowered his gaze whenever they had meetings in strip clubs. Which was quite often since Jax usually set them up.

"You want her?" Snake offered, raising his eyebrows again. He had already had her and could vouch for how warm and comfy she was inside. If not for her nasty pill addiction she would have made a nice addition to his rotation of side chicks.

"Huh? Oh, nah. I'm good. Let's get down to business," he replied once again. This time his partner did kick him under the table. "After we get our drink on of course!"

The waitress returned with a large bottle of cognac and poured each a drink. She looked to XL to see if he was drinking, and saw he was in mean mug mode. She shrugged and handed the men their drinks.

"My partner here wants to eat you from the back," Snake snitched. She shot her head to the guest to see which one he meant. Jax was smiling and nodding while Tonto was still

17

staring at the girl on stage. It was purely clinical as he watched his sister shake and shimmy for dollars. Maria was high as a kite and horny from men rubbing her vagina as they put money in her garter.

"He can," she smiled and gave him a booty shaking display as she walked away.

"I will!" he shouted and laughed after her. Snake ordered a few strippers to provide table dances while they sipped the Henny. Maria finally left the stage and Tonto mentally joined the others.

"Let's slide into a private room," Snake said ready to talk business. He gave XL a nod setting the extra-large man in motion towards the private VIP rooms. The men followed, followed by hand selected strippers.

Rohan was on high alert as they entered the plush back room. This wasn't a buy, so they weren't expected to have cash but he still stayed on point. Meanwhile, his young partner was straight clubbing. He groped one stripper's breast and another's ass. XL posted up at the door where he would remain while his boss handled business.

"Nile, why don't you take care of my friend Tonto here?" Snake asked even though he wasn't asking. The Egyptian woman quickly swooped between his legs and went for his zipper.

"Whoa!" Rohan protested and swatted her small copper colored hand away.

"You being rude!" Jax snapped in a tone matching Snake's expression. A Russian stripper knelt before him like an altar as he unzipped his pants and passed her his meat.

This was part of the job that the happy husband hated. Being undercover required him to indulge in forbidden acts. He didn't drink in real life but had to as Tonto. Rohan didn't use drugs but Tonto had to smoke weed, snort coke and pop a pill from time to time. Now he had no choice but to let the strange woman go down on him.

"That's better. Making me, mmm, feel some kinda way," Snake said as a sexy Honduran took him inside her warm mouth.

"I like to handle business and pleasure separately," Rohan explained trying to ignore what was happening below his waist. He could ignore it all he liked because his penis didn't need his permission to grow stiff. He looked to his partner slamming the woman's head up and down in his lap while thrusting his hips upward.

The room went otherwise silent, save the slurps and moans of the simultaneous blow jobs. One by one they came to grunting halts and gulps. Rohan held out as long as he could but even Superman wasn't immune to head. Likewise, head was kryptonite to many a married man.

A heaping dose of guilt chased the explosive pleasure like an early afternoon shadow. Rohan let out a heavy sigh as he put his deflating dick back where it belonged after being where it had no business. He sighed again thinking how to make it up to his wife even though she wouldn't know. She had quite a few gifts and trinkets from situations like this. She had a whole jewelry box filled from when they took down a prostitution ring out in Staten Island.

"Enjoyed that trip up the Nile?" Snake asked knowingly since he'd made that journey several times himself.

"Hell yeah! Now, about the dope," he said as the strippers cleared the room.

"About the dope. Like I told ya boy Jax, we don't deal in ounces and quarters. Ten bricks, at 19, then we front you ten more bricks. This is weekly, so if you ain't got the clientele say hell no," he said finishing the sentence in his Biggie Smalls voice from The Ten Crack Commandments.

"Shit, we can do twenty bricks in a day!" Jax cheered, getting a look from his partner. It said, 'calm down' so he did. "Twenty bricks a week is no problem."

"None at all. The price, however, is a problem. I can get it from the Mexicans or Dominicans for 17.5. Why would I pay extra?" Rohan asked even though he knew the answer. Snake was pretending to be the man when in fact he was just a middle man. Once they slapped the cuffs on him he would eagerly trade up to his connect. The dope game is proof that shit rolls uphill too.

"We can do 18.5," he quickly countered, hoping to hold onto his profit. He was scraping a grand or two off each kilo which added up to a pretty penny with all the bricks they moved.

"To start. 18.5 on purchased, 17.5 on the consignment," Jax tossed in. He was as shrewd as any real dope boy because he was a real dope boy. He swiped as much drugs as he could from every transaction and had a small team of dealers pushing his product.

"Eighteen on consignment and you got a deal," Snake agreed, looking between the two men. The fifteen grand a week was cool but something didn't sit well. Why was the sidekick handling negotiations? He wished XL would speak up during a deal.

"Deal!" Rohan agreed and stood to shake on it. He locked eyes with the dealer as they shook. Eye contact is like a human lie detector. Sure, some people can look you in the eye and lie but most can't.

"I hope you brought us a sample of what we're getting?" Jax asked hopefully. Half would go to evidence and the other half up his nose. Once they copped the bricks he would replace ten percent of the pure coke with cut and put it on the streets.

Rohan pressed his lips together to keep his protest inside as the dealer passed his partner what looked to be about an ounce of dope in a plastic bag. He was a vet and could weigh most drugs by eye. Had he been a betting man he would bet it wouldn't make it into evidence. As slick as Jax thought he was, Rohan was hip. He followed the cop code and kept silent knowing it would one day catch up with him. There was a special prison upstate for crooked cop, rogue judges and other officials gone bad. His partner was making reservations and it was time they parted ways. Once Snake was finally cuffed he could get his promotion and move on.

"You guys don't want to stick around? Sample some more flavors?" Snake offered.

"Sure. No thanks," the partners offered with equal enthusiasm. They both looked at the other wondering what the hell was wrong with the other.

"I got a thing, early," Rohan explained and begged off.

"Yeah, me too," Jax cosigned halfheartedly. There was a little cop in him and since they came together they would leave together. That didn't mean he couldn't come back later. The blow job was a nice appetizer but he was eager for an entree. Who could blame him when women from thirty countries were on the menu. Hands were shook and they made their departure.

Rohan zoned in on the door just as eager to leave as his partner was to stay. His tunnel vision caused him to walk straight into the back of a stripper. He was definitely going to smell like baby oil and have glitter on his face now.

"Shit!" he fussed more at himself than the woman since he assumed correctly that he and his partner had eyes on their backs.

"Watch where the fuck you...Rohan?" the angry stripper began with alcohol on her breath. She cut the tirade short seeing her big brother. Her initial reaction was glee so she wrapped her arms around him and kissed his face. Her second thought was, "What you doing here? I'm grown and..."

"I'll have to talk to you later. I'll call you," he urged and resumed his mission towards the door.

"Yo, Tonto, we can both hit that! She was on your nut sack!" Jax said. She was high on his list from her performance on the stage. He wouldn't mind holding those long Pocahontas braids while digging her out from the back.

"Stay away from her! Far, far away from her!" Rohan grunted getting in his face. He regained his composure a split second later and resumed his march to the door.

"OK, OK. I swear you Indian dudes don't like no black niggers messing with your women. But you married a black girl," Jax complained all the way out to the car. Rohan ignored his grumbles all the way back to the precinct.

Chapter 3

"You peep that shit?" Snake asked, scrunching his face into a question mark.

"See what?" XL asked unsure if he meant the exchange between Rohan and Pocahontas. He'd seen it but made nothing of it. After all, this was a strip club and dudes talked to strippers in strip clubs.

"Nothing," he replied assuming correctly that he wouldn't understand anyway. He'd been hired for his brawn not his brain. He was also good for reaching stuff on top shelves and heavy lifting but useless beyond that. "Bring me that Indian bitch."

"Which one?" he asked since they had several Indian wannabes. Give a chick a silky perm and she'd swear she had some Cherokee in her. Truth be told the only time they had some Indian in them was when the chiefs came down from the reservations upstate to trick off some of the tribes' casino money.

"The one you looking at!" Snake barked sending him off with a jump as if he'd been kicked in the seat of his pants. He watched as he rolled up on the girl in the middle of a table dance.

"Snake wants you!" he demanded, stopping her in mid shimmy. He used his big hand to summon another dancer to appease the grumbling customer. He removed a fifty from his pocket and handed it to the substitute stripper. "It's on me."

"I'm in trouble?" Maria asked as she followed XL to the back of the club. The club had a strict no tricking policy that most girls broke nightly; especially Maria. Her drug problem burned through cash at an incredible clip. He didn't know so he shrugged his broad shoulders in reply. Snake walked back to the private VIP room knowing they would follow.

"This one?" XL asked as he delivered the stripper. He received a dismissive wave and backed out of the door.

"I'm in trouble?" she asked again and pouted her lips in offering. She was pretty sure she could fix whatever she'd broken with a good blow job.

"Are you? What did you do?" he asked knowing she tricked. Most did so he had them tricking for him. "I saw how you worked it on stage and wanted a private dance."

"Oh, okay!" she giggled and began to sway her curvy hips. Snake leaned back and sipped his cognac to enjoy the show. And what a show it was.

Maria revealed her chest, one big brown titty at time. Her huge brown nipples gave him an infantile flashback, so he leaned forward and took one in his mouth. Then he reached between her legs and got nectar all over his fingers. His dick grew stiff and long despite just recently having been sucked off.

"Yo, who was that dude you were talking to on his way out?" he asked, massaging her love button when it popped out its hoodie.

"Mmm, which one?" she moaned. She'd talked to a bunch of dudes on their way out, plus she was high as a space station.

"Tonto, the Indian dude," he added, sliding a finger inside her bald, slippery box. She gave it a squeeze and giggled at his reaction. Any vagina that can squeeze a finger that tight is some good vagina.

"Rohan? My brother. He thinks he runs me since he's a cop" she said, twisting her lips. Snake was too cool to react visibly so he kept running his finger in and out of her.

"Mph, Jax too?" he asked, reaching into his pocket to retrieve a condom. He handed it to her when she reached for it and slid his pants down to his knees.

"I don't know who he is. His partner is an old white dude," she replied recalling his last partner. She opened the condom with her teeth then put it on him with her mouth.

"Mph," he repeated as he pulled her onto his lap. She reached down and guided him into her wet spot and eased down on it. Snake alternated between enjoying her vagina and thinking about his dilemma. He'd just made a deal with an undercover cop whose sister had some really good pussy.

His thoughts went to Jax and he wondered if he too was friend or foe. He certainly seemed like a crook, so what was he doing with the cop? Was he being set up as well or was he part of the setup? He was about to get his answer when XL knocked on the door.

"Boss?" he called, tapping again before opening and sticking his head in. He closed his eyes when he saw the girl straddling him and relayed, "Jax just walked back in."

"Take him to my table and have him wait. I want you to drive her home once we finish in here," he instructed never interrupting his stroke. He increased his stroke as soon as the door closed.

That was just fine with Maria who loved the sex, drugs and hip hop that was her life. It was a far cry from the Catholic schools and churches of her youth. Now, she preferred rough sex like the upward thrusts she was getting at the moment. The race to climax was close with her coming just ahead of him. They groaned and moaned in the shivering aftermath until he announced the end of the episode.

"Get up. I got business," he said, lifting her off his lap before even going soft.

"Aww," she pouted wanting to go another round or two. She settled for a pat on her ass and got up. She put her outfit back on to go dance some more while he removed the condom, wiped, and tucked his wood away.

"Wait here. XL will drop you off. I'ma fall through later and finish what we started."

"Ok!" she eagerly agreed since he tipped her so well the last time they'd hooked up. Not to mention his dick game was ridiculous. Snake slithered out the room and found XL and Jax sitting at his table. The bodyguard stood and rushed over to be told what to do.

"Take her up to Hunts Point and kill her. Then call whoever we know in Brooklyn and find out everything we know about Jax. Leave some room in the dumpster just in case he don't check out."

"OK," the large man said because what more needed to be said. He had his instructions and turned to carry them out. Snake put a fake smile on his face and slithered over to Jax.

"Sup 'potna! I had to duck dad and come back and see what you talking 'bout," Jax explained as he stood for a pound and hug.

"Yeah, your boy a bit stiff. How y'all know each other again?" he asked. His attempt to be nonchalant was wasted on the trained cop. Jax wasn't a very good cop, but he was trained if nothing else. Something was wrong and it was life and death that he figured out what.

"My mans put him on since he was moving a little work," Jax explained, pulling off nonchalant perfectly as he retrieved his stash of coke. The criminal watched closely as the cop inhaled a heavy hit in each nostril. He sure looked like a criminal to him.

"Why not?" Snake asked when he passed the coke to him. He normally didn't get high on his own supply but since he'd given it to the kid he made an exception. Besides, he wanted to see if it was really coke or Goody Powder. A real cop wouldn't actually use drugs. He took a light bump and explained, "Wife might want some wood later."

"I don't have them problems," Jax laughed. He could snort coke all day and stay hard all night. "Speaking of which, sup with that Indian broad? I sure wanna run up in that!"

"She's, indisposed at the moment," he replied at the same moment XL was choking the life out of her. He followed directions to a T and dumped her in a dumpster. He made sure there was plenty of room for one more, then made some calls as he headed back to the club.

"Well, what about the waitress? The one who brought us our drinks?" he asked since she would do too.

"Who Dominique? She ain't gonna do nothing," Snake answered. The girl talked shit but liked pussy just as much as Jax did if not more. "Pick one, any one."

"Hmm..." he hummed thoughtfully as he scanned the club fill of women. A child in a candy store if ever there was one. It was a close call but the little Thai thing working the pole edged out the Eskimo and Zimbabwean. "Her!"

"Nice choice!" Snake said and nodded since he'd sampled her tiny brown cheeks himself a few times. XL texted when he returned, so he called Dominique over so he could excuse himself. "Call Ming over when she finishes on stage and get them whatever they want. I'll be right back."

"That's a bet," the sexy waitress agreed and he was off. As soon as he was gone she leaned in and confided, "Ming pussy tastes like curry."

"How you...never mind. Shit you need to come with me, " he invited since it was the more the merrier when it came to freaks.

"Next time," she said and meant it when she saw him snort from the bag. "What you drinking?"

"May as well stick with the Hen-dog," he reasoned since it's what he'd started on.

"Well?" Snake asked irritably when he reached XL in the back.

"He checked out. I talked to Clay from Brownsville. Clark from Marcy and Big Reef from Bed-Stuy. All them know of him and have sold to him. He runs a crew of youngins and they getting money," he reported.

"Well, damn," Snake said hoping he hadn't kill the girl for nothing. "So, what about Tonto? What they saying about him?"

"No one knows him? Never heard of him," he replied with a curious shrug. "It's hard to get money in the streets of New York and no one hear of you."

"Not hard, impossible. That nigga is the police!" Snake said making his official declaration. The smart thing to do would be to shut down and not sell him anything. However, Snake was far from smart so instead said, " Let's kill him too."

"And dude?" XL asked, picturing the spot he'd picked out in the dumpster for Jax.

"Not yet. Matter fact, if dude is official I'ma let him kill him. He the one brought the nigga to me," Snake decided. He still needed that Brooklyn connect and Jax fit the bill. He would have to put in some work first though.

Jax was tossing back cognac with one hand and playing in Ming's pussy with the other when Snake and XL returned. The cop had got sidetrack by the slanted eyes and vagina until he saw the look in Snake's eye. A dead serious glint that reminded him of the danger.

"Everything okay?" Jax asked, mentally reaching for his pistol in case it wasn't.

"Yeah, yeah. Let's get out of here. Come on Ming," he said knowing he would follow. A true pussy hound will follow some snatch right over a cliff to his death. Get laid or die trying.

"Where we headed?" Jax asked as he followed Snake and Ming out the back door. Snake ignored the question until they pulled away and he asked again. Again, he was distracted when Ming began to massage his manhood through his pants. That wouldn't do at all so he leaned back and pulled it out. She popped it in her mouth like a Tic Tac and tried to suck the flavor out of it. He closed his eyes to enjoy the ride until it came to an end in front of a Bronx tenement building.

Jax was on alert when he saw some young goons standing in front of the building. They scattered and got somewhere when XL and Snake stepped out of the car. Jax breathed a sigh of relief and stepped out behind them. He helped Ming out since he hadn't hit yet. Dudes usually are perfect gentlemen until they hit. All decorum goes out the window after they nut. A chick will have to open her own doors after she opens her legs.

Jax followed them inside the building and up the stairs to a third-floor unit. XL used a set of keys and stepped aside to let them in. The level of comfort inside didn't quite match the outside letting him know this was one of Snake's personal spots. He had one himself down in Spanish Harlem. A spot to stash cash and side chicks until needed.

"Nice spot," Jax said, nodding in approval. Snake pulled a gun from his back in reply.

"Thanks. I decorated it myself," he said as Ming turned and left the apartment. XL pulled a gun next and the scene was set. Jax was strapped as well but held out to see if a diplomatic settlement could be reached. If not, he would go for his gun and they could all die.

"Sup yo?" he asked raising his hands. A position he practiced quick draw from on a regular basis at the range. He could pull both of the .40 Cals from his back in the blink of an eye but waited. If they wanted to kill him he would already be dead. He already had enough bodies under his belt to know this.

"Your partner is the police!" Snake said, cocking his head like a dare.

Part of being an undercover cop was acting and Jax was in the running for an Oscar. "Who? Tonto? Get the fuck outa here! Me and that dude been buying coke from that crew of Mexicans. I personally moved the work so I know it ain't in no police impound!" he insisted keeping a close eye on their eyes. People have a habit of squinting before they bust and both still had both eyes wide open.

"The Mexicans who got knocked off last month?" Snake asked with a humorless chuckle. Jax dug deep into his acting bag of tricks and found a perplexed mask and put it on.

"You right. And the Jamaicans before that. Oh shit! If that nigga is police he got everything on me! Shit, he ain't got shit on you since we never made a buy," he added so he realized he had a way out. He could call off the deal and go on with his life.

"I'ma ask you one time," Snake said with a squint that almost started a gunfight. Jax's hesitation would either get him rich or dead, but he was a gambling man. He gambled with dice, cards, lotto and even with his life by constantly running up in chicks raw. "Are you a cop?"

"No, I'm not! Ask anyone in Brooklyn about Jax Stacks! Only bad thing a nigga can say about me is I fucked his bitch!" he said quite convincingly. He saw he had him on the line and began to reel him in. "If you think I'm police then go on and buss. Shoot me if I'm a fucking cop!"

"Nah. I ain't gonna shoot you," Snake said and pursed his lips. He lowered his gun to his side since XL still had his aimed at his medulla oblongata.

"A'ight look. Fuck that cop! I'm the one with the street team. I'm the one actually moving the dope. He was just putting up the dough. I got my own dough and we can still do business," Jax offered. He'd planned on getting around to a side deal anyway to pad his pockets and contribute to his tricking.

"We can do that. Yeah, we can do that," Snake nodded. His tone and facial expression suggested more to it. There was and he added, "After, you kill that cop."

"Okay, but bring Ming back and you got a deal," he agreed like a really, really good actor.

Chapter 4

At the same time Jax was busy sticking his thing in Ming, his partner was back at the precinct busy catching up on their paperwork. Jax saw how much a stickler he was to cross T's and dot I's so he deliberately didn't, knowing his partner would take up the slack and do the extra work. That freed him up to pursue any one of his multiple vices. Rohan could have left for home at any time, but chose to give the city every second they were paying him for.

Once he wrapped up the paperwork, he went to take care of the perfume and glitter problem. The locker room had a shower for situations just like this. After all, police work was a dirty job; especially with all the dirty cops in circulation.

Rohan felt guilty as sin from his sin of letting the stripper blow him. He tried to write it off as just doing his job but hated how good it felt. The devil popped in his ear and tried to convince him that getting your dick sucked isn't technically cheating. He shook his head vigorously to remove the whispers because the devil is a liar. A married man shouldn't put his dick in anyone or anything other than his wife, period.

"Jamaica!" he announced as penance, since she just got a new vehicle. He had to do something to make amends for that fantastic blow job that threatened to make him hard again just thinking about it. He mentally told his dick to *hold that thought'* until he got home. Megan would be off to school so they could fuck on top of the bed with the door open instead of under the hot ass comforter behind a locked door. The thought made his foot heavy and sped the car up.

Rohan smiled and nodded in appreciation as he pulled into his driveway. He'd done well and provided a nice home for his family. Was he in over his head? Sure, but it was one of the best school districts in the state. His daughter wouldn't have to deal with the dirty, dangerous New York City schools he had to attend.

He hopped up the stairs as if he hadn't been up all night, the thought of his soft bed and some nice warm vagina having breathed new life in him. It would have been nice to have breakfast served when he walked in but he knew better. Michelle wasn't very domesticated but he accepted her flaws just like he accepted his own.

"That you?" Michelle called out groggily from staying up late drinking and watching TV. Good thing Megan was self-sufficient because her mother was hands off when he wasn't around. Megan knew how to fend for herself and get ready for school.

Michelle wasn't the best mom or wife but she would fuck her husband pretty much on demand. She had been using her vagina as a debit card since she was a teen. It was her only contribution to her comfortable lifestyle plus she was a bit of a freak. She loved to fuck which fooled Rohan into thinking he had a good wife who loved him.

"Yeah, I'm home," he replied with a grateful sigh as he entered their bedroom. All over the country one of his brothers in blue wouldn't make it home. It was open season on police now that people were tired of getting gunned down without a fight. Once it became crystal clear that black lives didn't matter, blue lives didn't either. The rallies and protest weren't working so they decided to clap back.

"How was your night?" she asked, reaching under her gown to rub herself. She may not have had breakfast ready but her pussy would be nice and slippery when he got in bed.

"Uneventful, same old thing. My new partner," he said shaking his head to complete the sentence. The blow job came to mind as he came out of his uniform. She watched in muted amusement as he neatly hung his clothes up. "We should go to Jamaica? I'm putting in for vacation once this case is over."

"You for real?" she popped up and cheered. She would just love to brag to Reese just as much as she would enjoy the trip. She would definitely visit her mother in the projects so she could show off her Caribbean tan. Not to mention stunt on all the dudes who stunted on her when she was young. All the ones who'd fucked her and left her. She'd turned the tables by marrying a cop and leaving them right there in the projects.

"Certainly! You're a good wife and Megan is a good kid," he said and slid into bed. He didn't notice the twist of her lips at the mention of taking their daughter along. Jamaica is different with kids or without kids. Michelle responded by dipping under the covers and taking him into her mouth. Rohan tried to enjoy the blow job but his guilt got in the way.

"I want to make love to you," he explained as he pulled her up. He rolled on top of her and she reached down to guide him inside of her. He had almost the same feeling as he did when he did when he pulled up into the driveway.

No, Michelle wasn't the best cook, homemaker or mother but boy could she fuck. She wasn't one of those women who lay there and let the man do all the work. No, she wiggled, squeezed, threw it back, clawed at his back and talked shit in his ear. His mother wanted him to marry a good Indian girl but once he got a taste of some hot, black vagina there was no going back.

"Fuck me!" she demanded when she felt an orgasm creeping into her life. She reached down and pulled her legs up and open so he could pound out a nut for them both.

Rohan knew the end was near and threw his hips into overdrive. He added a little grind to his down stroke just like she'd trained him. He didn't have the biggest dick, but she'd taught him how to sling what he had to get her off each and every time. Their lovemaking was a mutually beneficial cooperative like a good business venture. A win/win when they both got to come. A minute later they both contorted their faces and convulsed in pleasure. She squeezed as she felt him throbbing inside of her. He hoped to make that son he'd been wanting but the pill she took every day made sure that wouldn't happen. She once wanted a houseful of kids but now realized more kids would mean less money for her to shop with.

"Whew!" he said rolling off her. She popped up and retrieved a warm wash cloth to clean them both. She planted grateful kisses all over his brown face as he blinked and yawned. The overnight shift finally got the best of him and he drifted off to sleep. Michelle curled up next to him and joined him in dreamland.

****

"This bitch," Michelle muttered when her mother-in-law's name appeared on the caller ID several hours later. She wanted to love the woman, but the woman showed her absolutely no love. The old school Indian woman wanted her children to marry other Indians. She claimed not to be racist; she just didn't care for people of other races. So, she didn't hate Michelle for being black; she hated her for not being Indian.

It was bad enough when Maria started dating black guys, then her son turned around and married a black woman. Even had a black child and she wanted no parts of it. Said so too at their wedding. Wailed and shouted until she had to be removed. The phone rang itself out and went to voicemail. It wasn't what the old woman called for so she hung up and called right back.

"Hmp" she huffed, turning her nose up at the thought of answering it. Rohan began to stir when it rang a fifth time so she picked it up rather than let it wake him up.

"Rohan is sleep. We just finished making love, again and he's knocked out," she blurted and snickered when she took the call.

Bad Cop

"Tell him that his sister is dead," she said smugly. "She was found in a dumpster. Tell him that."

"Oh, Mrs. Mahatma, I ..."Michelle began to apologize but the line was dead. She realized her little ploy backfired and now she would have to deliver the grim news. Not to mention she genuinely liked Maria. They always found a way to sneak and smoke a blunt whenever she came to visit. That wasn't often since she and Rohan were always at odds. He refused to accept her chosen lifestyle as dope fiend, thot.

Michelle let out a deep sigh as she stood over her sleeping husband. She tried to figure out which angle to deliver the bad news with the softest impact. It came to her when he rolled and his dick peeped out of his boxer shorts. Nothing softens a blow like a blow job so she climbed on the bed and gave him one.

Rohan dreamed he was back in the club getting head from the stripper. He realized he wasn't sleep and this was no dream. He opened his eyes to make sure he was at home then looked down and made sure it was his wife. Michelle didn't go down town often because she sucked so much dick growing up, but when she did it was worth the wait. He leaned up on his elbows to watch the show like a selfie porn.

Michelle wanted to prolong the blow job as long as possible, knowing what would come after he did. It wasn't possible for him to withstand that bomb ass head for long and soon his legs began to shift. His moans increased and his head lolled back and forth. She braced herself and he exploded on her tonsils.

40

"Good morning!" he cheered once his breathing returned to normal. He didn't go downtown much either but was ready to return the favor. It was the least he could do after last night.

"Call your mom. She called a few times. I think something is wrong," she said unable to be the bearer of news that bad.

Rohan twisted his lips dubiously, knowing the blow job was part of whatever was going on. He let out a sigh and picked up the phone. Michelle sometimes forgets her husband was an actual detective. She remembered when he checked the call log and pursed his lips at the multiple calls. He remained silent since he knew the most important women in his life despised each other. He also knew there was nothing he could do about it. If a decade couldn't soften his mother's heart nothing would. Not even her beautiful granddaughter, Megan, was enough to break the glacier surrounding her heart.

"Did that black woman tell you what I said?" she dared knowing she hadn't and hoping it would cause trouble.

"No?" he replied, looking at Michelle who looked guilty. She lowered her gaze and let out a sigh at what she knew was coming. She was there to do whatever he needed in his time of need. To include breakfast, a shoulder to cry on, more head or some pussy if it helped.

"Your sister is dead! She was in the garbage. They found her when..." Rohan tuned out the rest of her rant and digested the grim news. He had been expecting it for years but it still hit harder than he expected.

"I'm on my way into the city now," he croaked when he cut in on her complaints about Maria's lifestyle and choice of men. Luckily Maria's daughter, Angel, had already been living with her grandmother.

"I'm sorry," Michelle offered on several fronts. She batted her eyes hoping for a tear and stroked his hand.

"I um..." he started and stopped when no further words came. He accepted her hand and found some comfort in it.

"Want me to come into the city with you?" she asked, ready to get fly and ride in with him. Even if it meant dealing with that nasty old lady.

"No. I, um..." he replied still unable to make whole sentences. "Megan will be home alone."

"Well let me make you some lunch. Take your shower," she said taking control. She poured a drink as soon as the water began to run. She sipped and made him a nice stuffed wrap of turkey and salad knowing he would want to eat on the run.

"I'm not going to have time to..." he began but was cut off by the outstretched meal to go. He smiled softly and sighed at her thoughtful gesture. The portable meal and drink killed all excuses. "Thank you."

"You're welcome, baby," she replied. She knew he smelled the liquor on her breath when he leaned in for a kiss but didn't complain, this time.

Rohan picked up his phone to call his partner out of habit. All his years on the force it had become second nature to call your partner when there was an issue. Being partners with Jax changed all that. He tossed the phone aside and opened his lunch. Forty minutes later he reached the Bronx and headed for the precinct.

"Detective Robinson," Rohan announced as he entered the foreign precinct. He always felt a tinge of grief at abandoning his family name of Mahatma, but knew he would go further with an Anglo name. Besides he'd been teased so bad as a child he secretly hated the name.

"Hey, Robinson, we been expecting you. Sorry 'bout your loss," a fellow detective said minus any remorse in his voice. It wasn't his fault that the city served up so many corpses he had become immune to it. Even pretty girls left in dumpsters didn't register.

"What do we know?" he asked, following him to his desk and taking a seat.

"Nothing. She was found at the dump when the trash guy emptied his truck. The crime scene is as contaminated as they come. Did she have a boyfriend? Enemies?" he asked looking for an angle to investigate. He saw no need in relaying the information about the three different semen samples found on and in the dearly departed.

"Boyfriend..." Rohan sighed remembering when that was the least of her problems. Back in the days she would date dope boys, then she began shaking her ass for them in the clubs.

Her daughter's father came to mind and he shook his head. Robert was actually a good Indian guy, but once Maria came up pregnant he got in the wind. It was ironic that the man her mother so desperately wanted for her was the one who shoved her into the beds and backseats of black men. He now lived down in Atlanta with his wife and other children. A collage of faces passed in front of his face, like a pull of a slot machine, but didn't stop on any one in particular.

"She worked, well danced, in club Back Shot over on Pelham parkway," he offered.

"Back Shots," the cop nodded thoughtfully. The place was well known to several departments within the department. Homicide, theft, prostitution and credit card fraud were common occurrences emanating from the establishment. "That'll be ground zero then."

'For me too,' Rohan thought to himself since he planned to work the case on his own. Dead strippers aren't worked with the same zeal as dead white people and it would grow cold by tomorrow. The other cop knew what he was thinking and was cool with it. It was his case so he would get the credit no matter who solved it. They stood, shook hands and parted ways.

Chapter 5

I don't think women are supposed to see men cry. It's unnatural, like seeing a cat bark, or pigs fly or something. I never saw my father cry until my Aunt Maria died. Although, I understood his pain the tears still shook me up. They made my heart hard and I can't recall crying ever since then. What I do remember was the anger. A raging hatred at whatever hurt my daddy. That's probably the day I decided I wanted to be a police officer. Some bad man hurt my daddy and I wanted to put all bad people in jail. It's funny now because I had no idea just how many bad people were out there.

Rohan let out a frustrated sigh as he neared the projects he grew up in. Anyone who ever escaped any projects, anywhere would know why. The projects are a place to leave, not go. It killed him that his stubborn mother refused to move out of them. Even when he extended the offer to move in with his family she still refused. Refused to live with the black woman and eat black people food. He shook his head at the familiar faces in the exact same places doing the exact same thing when he fled a lifetime ago.

A host of younger faces had replaced the old and the dead ones. They sat on those same benches slinging the drug of the era as if no one had done so before them. However, some of their parents had left butt prints where they now sat. The difference being they'd sold smack and crack where now they sold opioids and loud. The new dealers all got high on their own supply just like their predecessors.

"Rohan? Boy, you ain't changed a bit," an older lady exclaimed and clapped her hands when Rohan emerged from his vehicle. She often patrolled the parking lot trying to sell toothless blow jobs at a discount before they could reach the buildings where younger thots rented vagina for weed and club money.

"Um..." he replied, straining to place the weathered face. He assumed she was his mother's age until she spoke again.

"Anitra! We went to high school. 'Member?" she asked and showed him her gums.

"Wow!" he exclaimed as he realized who she was. She was once the baddest chick in the projects but now she just looked bad. As sad a sight as she was he still had a much sadder agenda in front of him. She made her sales pitch to his departing back as he rushed away.

"Ten percent off! I usually charge twenty, but for you 18!" She pleaded in search of financing her next fix.

"Whew!" he grimaced when the stench of stale urine assaulted his nostrils. He took a deep breath and rushed up the stairs to the third floor. Sounds of sex floated in the stairwell above as some teens became baby mama and daddy. He let his breath out when he finally exited on his mother's floor. He traipsed down the shrill hallway smelling like several different countries. Mrs. Johnson had some collards and fat back boiling, while the Yi families' kimchi battled for airspace. He knew the curry coming from down the hall was his mother's. He still had his key and used it to enter.

"Rohan?" Mrs. Mahatma asked fearfully as she clutched her pearls. For some reason, she just knew one of the black men wanted some of her old East Indian cookies.

"Yeah, it's me, Mom," he replied. She hoisted herself up and threw her arms open to embrace him.

"They killed my Maria! Those dirty black bastards killed my baby!" she fussed. Rohan twisted his lips ruefully since she didn't know who'd killed his sister. For all she knew it could have been an Indian or Jamaican or Vietnamese. He did know her hatred of black people extended to his wife and daughter. It's almost hard to love someone who hates people you love so he wouldn't allow it to consume his thoughts. Instead he pretended like all was well.

"I'll be working her case," he offered, even if it wasn't official. "I'll make sure whoever did this pays for it."

"I know you will, baby. You're a good son," she said, touching his face.

"Where's Angel?" he asked looking around for his niece.

"At school. Now, I have to tell her, her mother was killed by a black man," she lamented. He let out a sigh but held his tongue. His phone vibrated and he frowned down at the screen. Curiosity got the best of him so he answered the call despite what curiosity did to that cat.

"Hello?" he asked, instead of greeted, as he took the call.

"Sup yo? What's this I'm hearing about your sister?" Jax asked proving cop gossip just as much as everybody else. He took a swig of beer, pull on his reefer while making lines out of the cocaine on the table in front of him.

"Yeah, remember the Indian girl from the club last night? Someone killed her," he replied.

"Pocahontas? That was your sister! Oh shit, I'm sorry, bruh. Take the day off. I'll handle the business with Snake," he said relieved. This would eliminate him from the picture all together.

"Yeah. I um…guess I um…should," he acquiesced. He hated taking time off but needed to take time to bury his baby sister.

****

Rohan had been so deep in thought the drive home barely registered until he pulled into his driveway. Now the autopilot was off he had to deal with the here and now of the present. For him that meant admitting he'd failed in his duties and his sister was dead because of it. He was the big brother and it was his job to save her. He'd promised their father on his death bed to take care of her and their and he'd failed. Not that he hadn't tried, because he had. He'd taken beat downs and been shot at coming up trying to rescue his sister from herself. Self-destruction is the only destruction that can't be solved externally. It and self-esteem had to be handled in house.

"Oh Maria!" he wailed as deep heart wrenching sobs overcame him. Snot mixed with the tears and soaked his face. His chest heaved as animalistic sounds emanated from his soul. He would have drowned in his own tears if he hadn't looked up and saw his daughter's face. The look of sheer horror on her face shut the water works off immediately. He wiped his face with his hand and opened the car door.

"What's wrong, Daddy?" Megan asked in a panic. Obviously, the world was ending if Superman was shedding tears. Tears now streamed from her eyes as well.

"Nothing, baby. I'm OK. Let's go inside," he said trying to console her. He knew then that Michelle had saved the bad news for him. His baby girl was overweight from being spoiled, but he still managed to scoop her up and carry her inside.

"Here we go," Michelle muttered under her breath when they entered the house. The child had been fussing about where her father was since she walked in. She'd finally told her to go outside and wait for him. She was being sarcastic as usual but the girl did just that, despite the cool fall air. "Hey, baby. Are you OK? How's your mom holding up? And Angel?"

"What's going on, Daddy?" Megan now insisted. She put her hands on her chubby hips and put her foot down exactly like her mother would.

"Something happened to your Aunt Maria. She died," he explained as softly as he could. It's hard to console someone when you're in need of consoling yourself, but it's a parental duty so he did it.

"Was she sick?" the little girl asked, trying to reconcile the loss of life. Her pretty face scrunched up like it did when perplexed about something.

"Someone killed her," Michelle tossed in from across the room. She felt for her husband but hoped this didn't interfere with their trip to Jamaica. They both knew the loose woman was on the fast track to the morgue so it shouldn't fuck up her vacation.

"But why?" the child pleaded, needing an explanation. Being a smart child, she was used to there being a reason and explanation for everything.

"I don't know yet, but I will find out," he assured her.

"They're letting you work the case?" his wife reeled. Even she knew that would be a conflict of interest since she was his sister.

"Not officially, but..." he said not wanting to lie to either. "Let's go out to eat. I'm sure your mom needs a break."

"The buffet?" Megan asked hopefully. She loved to eat all she could eat from the all you can eat restaurant; especially the desert bar.

"No. We always go there. I'm in the mood for..." Michelle began but didn't make it to the end of her sentence.

"The buffet is fine," he cut in. He didn't realize it but always catering to his daughter over his wife caused jealousy. He'd failed at the balancing act and inadvertently made them compete for his favor.

Michelle sucked her teeth and stormed off to get dressed. The food was good but what upset her most was how was she supposed to brag to Reese about the all you can eat buffet.

****

Megan ate herself into a semi coma and had to be carried into the house when they made it home. That was fine by Michelle since it meant she could have him all to herself since he was taking the night off. She understood he was grieving and all but she was still horny.

Rohan grunted as he carried the heavy girl up to her room. He knew his spoiling her was the reason she was overweight but still couldn't say no to her. Men can ruin their daughters like this in more ways than one. She would have to sleep in her clothes since she was too old for him to change.

"Let's take a bath," Michelle offered when he returned from putting his daughter to bed. He would have declined but saw the candles flickering around the tub and didn't want to disappoint her either; especially since she'd slipped into a tiny nighty. He accepted his life of servitude to his family and his community.

"Sure," he agreed since a shot of booty would temporarily distract him from his failures. He sat on the bed and disrobed to join her.

Michelle selected the deep soaker tub when they'd remodeled for times just like this. The scented candles gave the ensuite a romantic glow and smell. The couple eased into the hot water at opposite ends. She took matters and the wash cloth into her hands. Rohan laid back to enjoy the water while she lathered the wash cloth and began to wash him. She started with his handsome face, neck and chest.

"Up," she instructed and he lifted his arms so she could wash underneath. She washed away the clumps of deodorant from his straight underarm hair and lathered the cloth once more.

"Mmm," he couldn't help but moan when she began to wash his genitals. She fondled and watched it grow hard and thick in her hand. It amazed her how he went from small while soft to a nice sized erection. She would have played Aqua woman and dipped below the water to give him some head but since he picked the buffet over where she wanted to eat he was dead on that.

"Move, a little, right there," she directed as she climbed on top of him. She reached down and wriggled him inside herself and sank down. She reached the bottom of his dick before she reached the bottom of her vagina and began to squeeze and rock. She popped a titty into his open mouth like a pacifier and he began to suck it. She rocked and squeezed, squeezed and rock until she came. "Mmm, let's get in bed so we can get it in!"

"OK," he agreed and got up after her. They dried off on the way to the bed and climbed in to make love. He went through all the motions even though his mind was miles away in the Bronx strip club, Back Shots.

Chapter 6

"Look at this clown," Snake said, shaking his head as Jax entered the club. He was supposed to be here on business but he was busy scoping and groping every woman he saw.

Jax was a real dick head in every sense of the term. The type of man who thinks with his dick instead of his head. A fuck first, ask questions last type of fellow. It depends on what a person believes if it was luck or divine decree that kept him alive.

"Yeah!" XL cosigned even though he wasn't exactly sure what he was looking at. He didn't catch a lot of his boss's words but didn't let on.

Jax was oblivious to the eyes watching as he tried to find a temporary home for his penis to spend the night in. He made up his mind on the way over to fuck each and every stripper in the club. It's good to set goals and that was his. He scanned the club like a kid in a candy shop trying to make a selection. When his gaze reached the VIP, he saw the men gazing back.

"Oh yeah!" he chuckled to himself and remembered why he was there. He adjusted his semi erection and headed off to take care of business. His inappropriate entry didn't even register as he greeted with a smile. "Sup fellas? Why the long faces? Who died?"

"Who didn't die?" Snake asked, twisting his face at the outstretched palm. He'd been watching the news looking for dead cops but found none.

"Bruh, I don't fuck with dude. I got a couple hundred grand in my trunk ready to do business. Good business. Killing police is bad business," he replied truthfully. "Killing niggers is acceptable, cool even but cops? Nah, you can't kill cops."

"But you can and you will," Snake growled with malice on his breath.

"Yeah," XL tossed in like a good hype man does. Jax didn't even glance his way since he was just a hype man. Instead he'd wait for the inevitable show down and gun his big ass down.

"Bruh, let's get this money. That cop ain't got shit on either one of us. Let's do some business and get rich," Jax pleaded.

"Nah. Here, enjoy," he replied, tossing him a baggie of chunky, beige cocaine. "That along with drinks and one of the girls are on me. A going away present cuz I don't wanna see you around here again while that cop is still breathing."

Jax had a fly response but had to hold on to it since Snake turned and walked away. He followed him with his eyes all the way out the club. After waiting and watching the door for several minutes, he accepted that he wasn't coming back. He shrugged and dug into his consolation prize. XL watched in muted disgust as his dumped some of the coke on the table. He crushed it and formed four thick lines before leaning in and inhaling them.

"Shit! This that shit!" he exclaimed and fell back rubbing his burning nose. He remembered the rest of his prizes and raised a hand for the waitress. The same pretty lesbian came over so he ordered the same cognac from before.

"Is that it?" she inquired before setting off.

"Nah, matter fact, who got the best tasting pussy in here?" he asked since it was on the house.

"Probably Reign. That pretty chick from Harlem," she said pointing at a slim, pretty woman working the stage.

"Bet. Send her to me once her set is over," he ordered and watched her ass shift as she walked away. He added her to his list too as he made more lines.

"Why don't you take that to a VIP room?" XL suggested since cocaine was still illegal. He wasn't the only patron snorting it but was the only one not trying to be discrete about it.

"Sure. Send the broad in," he agreed and took off. The waitress met him a moment later with a bottle and a couple of glasses. He grunted his thanks and fixed another line. Several songs later the door opened and in walked Reign.

"Sup yo?" she greeted, scanning the room and then him. Meanwhile Jax was scanning her from head to toe.

He nodded approvingly at her slim frame and small but pretty breast. They were firm and perky with delicious looking nipples. The plumpness of her vagina could clearly be seen beneath her colorful boy shorts.

"Sup with you? Bambi said you got the best tasting box in this joint."

"Did she?" she replied wondering how she would know since she'd never gotten a lick. They were cool enough for her to steer VIP customers in her direction. The cocaine on the table answered the question of why he was asking about edible pussy. After snorting all that fish scale no way was he getting an erection. Coke is kryptonite to a hard dick.

"She did and I wanna see for myself," he insisted. He tossed a stack of bills on the table to sweeten the deal. "Come out them clothes, sweetie."

"That's what's up," she said, weighing the cash by hand and nodding. She stepped back and out of her shorts as he took another swig and snort.

"Un uh. From the back," he corrected when she tried to sit on the table in front of him. Her face twisted into a 'huh?' but she shrugged and complied. She climbed on the table doggy style spread her legs and arched her back. It was a waste of the perfect back shot arch, for him anyway because she was in for a treat.

"My, my, my!" he said, marveling at the pretty, bald pussy. He had to save some for later and whipped out his phone. He took a few still shots to add to his enormous collection then shot a quick video while he fondled the glistening juice box. It bloomed and blossomed, soaking his fingers in that good nectar.

"Sss!" Reign hissed and arched her back even more when he flicked his tongue across her throbbing vagina. It was all the encouragement he needed to go to town. He peeled her ass cheeks open and went in. He twisted and twirled his tongue around her swollen clit until she filled his mouth with her juices. He swallowed it down and went for seconds, then thirds. They moved on to the sofa where he spread her legs to their limits and sucked a forth nut out of her.

They both checked his dick periodically but it was still limp and harmless from snorting coke all day. She enjoyed the tongue lashing but was ready for some dick. Unfortunately, none was coming. She did however. Over and over, in between and during snorts of coke and sip of cognac.

"So, you want my number? Maybe we can hang out or something?" Reign asked hopefully after XL called through the door announcing closing time. She stood on rubbery legs from multiple orgasm and got dressed.

"Nah, but I'll see you round," he declined since there were a hundred more girls to get to at the club. He chuckled at the disappointment on her face as he left. He nodded a phony farewell to XL and tossed a fake salute on his way out. He staggered drunk, high and bloated off pussy juice to his car. That's where he found his partner waiting.

****

"What the hell are you doing here?" he asked in a panic looking around to see who could see them. He was slightly relieved to see Snake's empty parking spot but XL would be out any second.

"I should be asking you the same thing?" Rohan shot back.

"Follow me," Jax insisted and got into his car. He rushed out of the parking lot watching to make sure his partner was behind him. He led the way down to a diner on 161st street and parked. A minute later they were seated inside.

"Well?" Rohan asked once a waitress filled their cups with black coffee. The smell of alcohol and pussy wafted across the table when he opened his mouth.

"Well, I spent all night trying to get this guy Snake to sell us some blow. Waste of time, he's just bluffing. He ain't got shit. Time to cut our losses and move on," he said while turning his coffee from black to light, bitter to sweet with a large amount of cream and sugar.

Rohan sipped his coffee like she'd bought it and processed the series of lies. He'd arrived at the club several hours ago just as Snake left and never returned. It was only the presence of Jax's car that made him stay instead of following. So, no way was he talking to him all night. Next, Snake definitely had drugs. No, he wasn't the connect but was directly connected to the connect.

"I see..." he said since none of it made sense. "Anyone say anything about my sister?"

"Your... no, you think? Nah, nothing," he replied finally catching on that there could be a connection between Snake discovering he was a cop and the fact they were related. He certainly was paranoid enough to kill her for being related to him. "Hmp?"

"What?" Rohan said seeing his mental moment of clarity.

"Huh? Nothing," he replied since he couldn't share it. It bothered him to let the million-dollar connection go, but he wasn't killing a cop; especially not his own partner. Maybe some random beat cop in Brooklyn but not his own partner.

"If there was would you tell me?" Rohan asked, leaning in to peer into his soul to see where his answer came from. Most people can't look a person directly in the eye and lie.

"Of course, I would!" Jax said looking him directly in his eyes and lying.

"Good, cuz I'm bringing that bastard down!" he vowed. Jax let out a frustrated sigh at the loss of millions he could've made with a decent plug. The only other way was killing a cop.

Chapter 7

I remember the first time I set eyes on Jax. Maybe it was because of the way he set his eyes on me. I can still recall the cold shiver that ran up my spine when we locked eyes. I knew in an instant he was trouble. I just had no idea just how much trouble he really was.

"Are you OK, Daddy?" Megan asked when she found her father in the den rocking back and forth while staring off into space. He was watching a mental movie of what ifs and should haves that could have saved his sister. However, all the second thoughts and hind sights in the world are no match against divine decree. Everything has already been written, the pen has been lifted and the ink has dried.

"No," he admitted to his own surprise. It had been his habit to hide and sugarcoat life's ugly moments from his pretty daughter. Today he had to bury his baby sister so no, he was not OK. "But, I will be. We all will be."

That was good enough to bring a smile to Megan's face. Sure, it was a sad occasion but she was still excited to see the pretty lady in the pictures she knew was her grandmother. There was always some reason or explanation as to why they could never visit her or her them. Not today though because they would all be in the same place at the same time.

"I can't wait to see my grandma and Angel!" she said happily as they walked through the house. She and Angel were close from her occasional visits with her mom. She was the same age but quite a bit more mature, fast actually. Megan got a giggling kick out of hearing the girl curse and confess to all the bad stuff she did in the city.

Michelle craned her hearing from the kitchen to hear his reply. She often wanted to tell her daughter the truth. The truth was that her racist old grandmother was a hateful old woman who hated black people.

"Sure," he replied since it was inevitable. He just hoped the somber setting would soften her hard heart.

"Hmp," Michelle huffed as she joined the procession out to the car. Rohan furrowed his brow meaning *chill* and she pursed her lips to reply a curt whatever. The couple often had tacit arguments like this in front of their sheltered child. Grownups arguing in front of children is a form of child abuse.

Sheltering a child is a double-edged sword. Sure, parents want to shield their children from life's shit, but this is life and shit happens. Shit some sheltered children won't be prepared for.

No one listened to the banter coming from the stereo as they rode into the city. Some goofy DJ made fun of celebrities who were doing way better in life than he was. That filled the empty space between brainless songs with empty lyrics and morally deficient messages. Today everyone was busy with their own thoughts.

Michelle was trying to figure out if she could get a husband to swing by her old projects to see her mom, so she could slip over to Reese's apartment to get a few tokes of whatever she was smoking on. Wouldn't it be wonderful if she had a few lines of blow on the cheap black lacquer coffee table? Her stomach rumbled in anxious anticipation.

Megan mentally played out the scene of meeting her grandmother and seeing her cousin. She played out each role in a different voice enjoying the happy reunion.

Rohan was analyzing every word, phrase and facial expression from Jax the previous night. The lies stood out even more the morning after but made even less sense. His partner wouldn't have had anything to do with his sister's death, but he knew it was somehow related to the club. The club was owned by Snake and Jax was lying for Snake. Those were the facts but nothing made sense beyond that.

Everyone replayed fond memories of Maria in better times, like when she was alive. Megan just loved how her pretty aunt always gushed over her. She called her pretty, not fatso like the kids in school. Michelle smiled softly as she recalled when she came out for a pool party a few months back. They'd snuck off and smoked weed on a run to the market. Rohan just remembered the sweet little girl she once was until puberty turned her into a woman and the streets turned her into a whore. They all let out individual sighs when they crossed over into the Bronx.

****

Park Lawn Cemetery is a sprawling green space uptown where the people of the Bronx buried their dead. The good, the bad and the ugly would all rest here until the trumpet is blown, and it's off for final judgement. There were several services going on simultaneously because death is a part of life.

The Mahatmas weren't Christians so there would be no church service. Instead they would cut through to the chase and meet at the gravesite.

A rented Hindu preacher blew his breath in frustration as he checked his watch. His time had already begun, but no one except the mother and daughter were present.

"I can start?" he offered so she could get his whole spiel in.

"My son is on the way. He's a police man," she replied. Ironically it was that same statement made by the girl in the box that got her put in the box. No sooner than the words came out she spied Rohan pulling to a stop. A smile began to form but died just as quick seeing the black people in the vehicle with him. Her hatred wouldn't allow her to accept her daughter-in-law and granddaughter as family. No, they were just black people to her.

"Hmm?" Rohan heard himself say as they reached the cemetery. He wondered where all the people were. Where were all those guys he had to fight in a futile attempt to keep them out of his sister? Where were all her so-called friends, who'd taken precedence over her family?

It was probably best no one did show up. The family would have been shocked and amazed at the array of men and women who'd found relief in between her legs and jaws. Amazed by the circus worthy collection of misfits who shared Maria's short time on earth before she was lowered into it.

"Mother," he greeted when he reached her side. She threw her puffy arms wide and wrapped them around her son. Megan smiled nervously at the woman who'd never set her eyes on her before.

The preacher took advantage of the moment and got to preaching. Angel reached a hand out to Megan who came over and took it. They both curiously watched the man speaking Hindu, wondering what the words meant.

"Psst," Michelle huffed at the slight to both her and her daughter. Had this been any other place or time she would have finally told the old woman off. Only out of respect for the dead did she hold her tongue.

Rohan only half listened as he scanned the area. He spotted an inappropriately dressed woman making her way over and assumed correctly she was friend of his sister. She lowered her head and listened intently even though she didn't understand a word. He decided to question her as soon as his sister was lowered into the ground.

Megan was amused by the Spanish woman in the high heels and tiny skirt. An even tinier top strained to hold her silicone breast inside. She saw her father staring at her and wondered if he would get in trouble like he did for looking at a woman in the mall a few months back. She looked at her mom who was mentally on the other side of town.

"My baby," Mrs. Mahatma wailed when it was time to lower the casket into its resting place. She could only hope the restless woman could finally found some peace.

"Here," Angel said sharing a few of her flowers so they could toss them in the hole. Megan accepted them just as another man approached. What stood out most about him was her father's reaction to his presence. He made that face he made when he was displeased about something.

"I'm sorry for your loss," Jax said giving his partner an unwelcome and uncomfortable hug. He took the opportunity to gawk at his wife and child while he hugged him.

Megan felt a chill as his eyes roamed her young body. They paused where her breast would one day be then dropped to her crotch area. When they met her eyes, she felt a shiver. He made a face like one does when reeling in a small fish before throwing it back then moved on to her mother. Michelle smiled flirtatiously when he looked her up and down the same way.

"What are you doing here?" Rohan asked once he freed himself from the awkward embrace.

"I had to come show my respects," he lied. He needed to steer his partner as far away from Back Shots as possible. He needed this connect and wasn't going to let his goody two shoes partner fuck it up for him.

"And..." Rohan whispered while watching his mother's mouth move in silent prayer.

"And, I got a lead on a major pill pusher down in Chelsea. That Snake biz didn't pan out," he offered, twisting up his face as if it left a bad taste. Rohan opened his mouth to reply but saw the Spanish woman cross herself and turn to leave.

"Excuse me," he said and took off after her. His long strides tracked her down before she got too far. Jax of course moved on his wife immediately.

"You must be Michelle," Jax greeted extending his hand. He immediately noticed her take notice of the ice on his fingers and neck and knew she was a gold digger who dug diamonds and gold. "I heard a lot about you."

"And you must be Jackson," she said accepting his hand. Jax gripped it, held it too long and peered into her eyes. He crossed the line by licking his lips seductively giving her a choice. She could pull away with dignity or stay and commit adultery. She made her choice by giving his hand a squeeze like she does with her vagina when her husband was on the verge of climax. A little nudge to push him over the cliff. They were still holding hands when Rohan reached the stripper.

"Excuse me. Ma'am?" he said, announcing his presence. "Did you know Maria?"

"Yes, we worked together," she said leaving out getting high together, turning tricks together, running credit card and bad checks together and occasionally coming together during sex.

"At Back Shots?" he asked assuming she was a stripper since she wasn't fully dressed even now at a funeral.

"Yeah. I was there with her the night she disappeared. Snake's cheap ass called her up to the private room. He makes me sick, always tryna fuck for free!" she frowned from having been fucked for free by him as well.

"And what happened when she came back?" he cut in so the last memory of his sister wouldn't be a free trick in a strip club.

"She never did. Pearl Tongue said she seen her go out the back door with XL. That don't make no since though cuz last thing he wants is some pussy," she replied.

"Pearl...Tongue?" Rohan asked wondering if that was a person, place or thing.

"Yeah, they call her that cuz she got a huge clit! Dudes be sucking on it on stage and..."

"And take my card and give me a call later," he cut in handing her his card. He heard his wife's laughter and saw she and Jax getting along famously. He wasn't jealous per se, but just didn't want the man near his family. She read 'police', frowned, then tucked it into her designer purse.

"OK," she decided since cops were the biggest tricks and had the best drugs in the city.

"I see you met my partner, who was just leaving," Rohan announced, breaking up their bonding session.

"Yeah, he was just telling me, and un uh..." she said feeling embarrassed by the dampness in her panties. The pretty young man reminded her of the pretty thugs she used to date before marrying the cop.

"OK. Anyway, get Megan so we can go," he said dismissing his wife so he could talk with his partner. "Got a lead on what happened to my sister. Let's meet at the office in a couple hours."

"Office? How about Chelsey? Like I said, I got wind of a new plug down there. We may be able to kill two birds with one stone," Jax replied, nodding to make his partner go along with it. He only did so because he saw his wife and daughter approaching his mother.

"OK, sure," he agreed over his shoulder and rushed off to chaperone the women. He hoped for the best but knew his mother enough to expect the worse.

"Oh, and I might, fuck your wife if you don't mind?" Jax asked with chuckle since he was out of ear shot. He had a mid-level pill dealer they could arrest so he could have Snake all to himself.

"So, Rohan said you cooked? He's always bragging on how good your food is," Michelle offered as an olive branch when she reached the old lady. Compliments usually make great ice breakers so she started with one. Poor Megan stared up hopefully, still waiting to be acknowledged.

"I didn't make enough for you," she said in a manner that made the innocuous words sound like curses. Luckily Rohan arrived just when he did because Michelle's mouth opened wide and she could curse with the best of them.

"Mom, be nice. Michelle came to show her respects for..." he pleaded but the nasty old woman turned and walked away. "I'm sorry, I.."

"Don't be. Go deal with your mama. I'm going to see mine," she said storming off. Rohan looked back and forth between his mother and wife. He shook his head and followed his mother. He reasoned she needed him most since she'd just lost a child. All Michelle knew was once again he'd chosen someone else over her.

"Go with your mom. I'll come over a little later," Rohan told his lingering daughter. She too would choose him over her mom if given a choice.

"OK, Daddy," 'she agreed since she didn't have a choice. She had to run to catch up because her mother would have left her. She and her father waved and blew each other a kiss until they saw each other again.

Chapter 8

"You wanna spend the night with your grandma?" Michelle heard herself ask as she drove across town. A whisper told her Rohan needed to be punished by her spending a night on the town. She was only being nice to Megan because she planned on being naughty tonight.

"No," she replied honestly. The projects were a far cry from the suburbs she was used to. The yelling, cursing, fighting and shooting was just too much on the sheltered girl. She was still amazed that her mom had actually once lived here.

"Well, you're going to cuz I'm going out!" she shot back since her mind was made up. She'd been a good girl for years so one night of being bad wouldn't hurt anyone; especially since her husband was a mama's boy who'd picked his mother over his wife. Whatever happened tonight was partly his fault. If she ended up in some man's bed it was Rohan who'd tucked her in.

"OK," Megan groaned as they entered the dirty projects. Young thugs peered at the new vehicle as it entered. They planned to steal it the second it parked to joyride in for the night. Luckily an old head announced the driver was alumni. People who made it out got a free pass to come and go if they left family behind. There was a little honor among thieves. Not much, but a little. An animalistic instinct not to shit where you eat.

Megan watched the strange people as they pulled in and parked. People didn't look like this out on the island and they didn't stare back like these people did. They were loud, colorful and expertly inserted curses into every sentence. Not everyone in the projects were crude; just the ones who hung out all day and night, smoking and drinking, fucking and fighting, living and dying in these streets.

"Stop looking at everyone," Michelle said as they walked to the building. Looking people in their faces can be construed as a challenge but the naive suburban girl didn't know any better. She called out to her childhood friends by name along the way. "Hey Black, Reef, Buddha."

"Oh, you don't see me, huh?" Ray-Ray asked, throwing his arms out wide.

"No!" she huffed and lifted her chin defiantly and marched inside.

Megan knew from previous visits to take a deep breath of outside air before stepping inside. She would have to hold it during the quick sprint up the pissy stairs to the second floor. Her mother's heels click clacked loudly in the shrill staircase as they ran up to her mother's apartment. They echoed in the hallowed hall down to the coveted end apartment. The end apartments were always the best because you could be nosey on two sides. Her grandmother's unit faced the parking lot and the courtyard making it one of the best seats in the house.

"Who?" Dianne yelled through the metal door in response to the knock. She reached for a tennis racket she kept near the door since she wasn't expecting company. The ancient racket hadn't hit a ball in decades but did bust a couple crack heads in their cracked heads on occasion.

"It's me, Ma!" she called back. The sound of multiple locks being unlocked could be heard outside in the hall. Michelle let out a silent sigh of relief at not having to live like this anymore. Now if she accidentally forgot to lock her doors a neighbor might come lock it for her. Maybe camp out on the front steps to protect the family. Maybe not but they certainly wouldn't come in and steal her shit.

"Look at my babies!" Dianne cheered, clapped and bounced from foot to foot. She rushed and embraced her daughter before she could even step inside.

"Hey, Ma," Michelle squealed as she relished in the love. She inhaled deeply to catch an aroma of what her mom was into these days. She smelled malt liquor and weed but not the dangerous drug that had kidnapped her mother for a few years. Dianne loved her only child more than anything else. Her grandchild came second which was fine by her. It was that love that helped her beat a nasty crack addiction and bounce back.

"And my pretty little grand baby," she said turning her affection on the child. The girl knew to hold her breath for the grandma's hug too, knowing the woman smelled like menthols and malt liquor.

"Hello, Grandmother," the proper child greeted properly.

"Grandmother," Dianne repeated and giggle. "My baby all bougie from growing up out there with them white folks! Probably eat mayonnaise and err thing!"

"Yeah, she does!" Michelle laughed as they all entered the projects. The room could have been a time machine because it was exactly the same as when she left over a decade earlier. The same as when she grew up here as a child. Both she and her daughter glanced around taking it in.

The cinder block always captured Megan's attention. She'd never been to prison but that's exactly what they reminded her of. She often heard her mother say she escaped from this place which only confirmed her suspicion that this was a prison. The gates around it were there to keep the residents in.

"You guys hungry?" the gracious host asked and lifted herself off the sofa. Her fridge was jam packed with everything food stamps could buy along with a few forties of her favorite brew.

"No thank you," Megan said politely because there were far too many roaches scurrying about for her liking.

"Yes!" her mother corrected. She was oblivious to the roaches and still loved her mother's fried chicken. The grease would soak up some of the alcohol she planned on drinking tonight. "Ma, I'm going out with Reese so I'ma let her spend the night with you. OK?"

"Reese, hmp!" she huffed indignantly, twisted her lips and shook her head.

"Oh Lord, what my girl done did now?" Michelle laughed knowing her wild friend was capable of anything.

"You mean who, and who ain't she did!" the woman cackled. She went on to explain how her friend was screwing everyone in sight. Some things never changed because she'd

74

been using her vagina as a credit card, weed card and bus pass since their teens.

Meanwhile, Megan posted up in the window, hiding behind the curtain so she could see but not be seen. The colorful project dwellers always fascinated her. A group of girls only slightly older than her talked, cursed and laughed loud enough to be noticed by the group of boys nearby. Some teens played ball while others slung dope to their aunts, uncles, moms and strangers.

She found herself mocking and imitating the animated girls.

"Un uh. I don't like dat nigga!" Megan repeated after a loud little girl below. She had her down to a T, with neck and eye rolls.

"What are you doing?" Michelle asked, laughing as she caught the tail end of her act.

"Nothing, Mommy. Are we going home now?" she replied and asked hopefully. There's no place like home in general but especially when visiting the projects.

"No, baby. You're staying with your grandma," she replied on her way to the door. "That means don't be calling your father to come get you."

"OK," she said to her wake as she departed the apartment.

"Don't pout, girl. It's about time we get to hang out. You know how to play Tonk?" Dianne asked retrieving a deck of cards.

"Who?" the girl asked of the unknown word. She always learned a new word or two when she visited the projects. She always found a way to work them into a conversation sooner or later.

"Bid Wiz? Spades? Gin Rummy? Come on, I'll teach you," she said and began to deal her in. "You got your allowance?"

****

Meanwhile, Michelle crossed the courtyard like a celebrity since she didn't have to live there anymore. She did enjoy coming through from time to time to stunt on those she'd left behind. The five-minute walk took fifteen as she greeted all those left behind. She made sure to shake her ass in front of the same dudes who'd once had it to show they could never get it again. These were the survivors who'd beat jail and death, for now.

"Who?" Reese called as she opened the door since she already knew who. Word is the only thing that spreads quicker than STDs in the projects.

"Me, bitch!" Michelle shouted as the door swung open. She caught a whiff of gas in the air and barged her way inside. She spied a blunt smoldering in the ashtray and made a beeline to it. It took priority over greetings and hugs.

"It's dir..." Reese tried to warn but it was a moot point when her guest took a deep drag. Michelle's eyes went wide when she tasted the cocaine lacing the weed. A taste she knew well enough to recognize immediately. She could have blown it out and been spared from its effects. Instead she shrugged and took sips of air to spread the drugs into her system.

"What, club...is...pop-popping...tonight?" she asked trying to keep the smoke in as long as possible.

"Shit, we can hit Jewels downtown, Maximum out in Queens, or, The Palace on 125th," she said, even though she was broke at the moment. She'd spent her spare cash on the drugs her friend was smoking. That's why she let her smoke so she could return the favor. "My money funny right now though. I just copped some get high cuz I was staying in."

"Shit, you sprang for the weed so I got you in the club," she offered just like she'd hoped.

Chapter 9

"I have to go now, Ma," Rohan announced hours after he arrived at his mother's house. He felt guilty and full of lamb Roti and all the fixings. The food was wonderful though so he packed a plate for his family.

"OK, baby. I'll mourn alone," she replied, heaping a heaving helping of guilt on him just like she did when fixing his plate. She'd hoped he would stretch out on the sofa and sleep like he used to. Like his dad use to before working himself to death.

"Or you and Angel can keep each other strong and take care of each other just like you've been doing," he shot back when his call came up empty. His wife was still sending him to voicemail so he gave up and summoned a ride. He shook off the thought of having his partner pick him up because he simply didn't trust the man. He knew the powers that be had assigned Jax to him to keep an eye on him. They knew full well he would report any criminal activity. Jax knew it too.

Mrs. Mahatma was still wailing and groaning as he left the apartment. She cut her act when she heard the elevator open and close. Being a phony old bat allowed her to turn her emotions on and off like a switch. Angel took note of her antics for use later in life.

The car service came and scooped Rohan up and headed towards Manhattan. It wasn't until they crossed the 159th street bridge that he called his partner.

"Sup yo?" Jax answered when he saw his partners name on his screen.

"Just leaving the Bronx," Rohan replied, putting the ball in his court. He was interested to see if he wanted to go with the bird in hand by trying to buy from Snake or this obvious wild goose chase down in Chelsea. The latter would be proof of collusion and he planned to press the issue. He cared nothing about the dope, he wanted whoever killed his sister behind bars.

"I'm downtown now," he lied from Brooklyn. Jax knew he could still arrive in lower Manhattan before his partner would if he was in the Bronx.

"And you're sure you don't want to try Snake again? He's on the verge of letting go of quite a few kilos," he pressed.

"Nah, he's not talking 'bout nothing. We can bag this pill guy and flip him," Jax said still trying to salvage the connect. A couple of years with a good connect would have him straight for life. Being a narcotics officer was the perfect way to protect his operations.

"OK. Where you wanna meet?" Rohan asked. He relayed the new destination to the driver and hung up. He tried his wife once again with the same results. This time he decided to leave a message. "Sorry, baby, I'll make it up to you. How's about a shopping trip before Jamaica?"

****

"Hmp!" Michelle huffed when his face popped up once again on her vibrating phone. She took a deep drag of the cocaine laced blunt, leaned back and sent him to voicemail once again.

"I know that's right, bitch. A nigga who chooses his moms over his wife needs to go to voicemail!" Reese cosigned. Her advice was negligible at best since she couldn't keep a man longer than it takes to bust a butt. A married woman should never take advice from their perpetually single friends. What could they know about maintaining a relationship? "Let his mom suck his damn dick!"

"Anyway, what's been happening around here since I been gone?" she asked to change the subject. She was hot but that was extra, even for her. Besides, she already had enough fodder to fuel her night out.

"Guuurl!" Reese began as if she had some juicy gossip to share. In the end, it turned out to be the same scandals she lived through when she lived here. What else could she expect in the hood except hood shit. An hour of who fucked who and who got killed by who. The only thing that had changed since she left was the hairstyles.

****

"Here I go!" Jax said raising a hand as Rohan entered the pizza shop. He nodded and made his way to the back of the restaurant where he was seated. Rohan scanned the dimly lit establishment for danger but none registered. He wondered for a second why he chose this spot but recalled dives like this often had the best food.

"OK, so tell me why you think Snake is a fake?" asked sliding into the booth across from him. "We negotiated a large buy with him and now..."

"Well, I asked around about him and no one can vouch for him. He's a middle man at best. Then I confirmed it that night I saw you outside. Waste of time. Now this guy Fresh has the opioid market on smash! We bust him and..."

"And you're lying!" Rohan cut in. "Let me tell you how I know. First, I watched Snake leave the club that night. Hours before you did so no way were you talking business with him. I'd put my money on you in a private room with your cock in one of the girls. Next, my sister was seen leaving the club with XL after spending time with Snake in a private room. He had her killed. Why?"

"Because she told him you're a cop. I'm trying to distance myself from you so I can still make the buy," Jax admitted, but the truth stopped there. "We can still bag this guy but I gotta convince him I didn't know you was a cop. You gotta fall back and let me work him."

"No, what I'm going to do is arrest him and XL for the murder of my sister. I'm going to arrest you too for obstruction if you get in my way," he dared.

There was a tense silence while both processed the moment and plotted the next move. Rohan played his hand so it what now Jax's move. His head began to nod slowly as he accepted the situation.

"Just getting my phone," he warned as he reached into his pocket. Rohan tensed in case he came out with anything else. Whoever he called must have been anticipating the call because they answered on the first ring. He casually relayed what he had to say and hung up. "Plan B."

"Which is?" Rohan asked curiously. He was even more curious when his own phone began to play the ring tone he set for his partner.

"Really!" Jax laughed as the old KRS-1 song Black Cop began to play. They locked eyes as he pressed the button to take the call and lifted the phone to his ear.

"Hello?" Rohan asked while maintaining eye contact with his partner. He wondered who was calling him from his phone when he was sitting right across from him in the booth. Just like that curious cat he was dying to find out.

"Plan B," the voice announced and hung up. Rohan held the phone to his ear to see if more was to come but none did.

"What are you doing?" he insisted, sitting his phone on the table.

"Setting up an alibi. I respect the whole *good cop* thing but I'm not one. I'm a bad cop. A black cop just like the song says," he replied as the front door of the restaurant opened. A man tugged his hoodie down to conceal his face and walked briskly towards the back. The patrons were too busy smashing some of the best pizza in the city to notice him. Jax wasn't though, he was expecting him.

"Alibi for what?" Rohan asked wanting to get that on tape too since he had been recording since he walked in the door.

"This," Jax said just as the man reached their table. He lifted a small caliber pistol to the back of Rohan's head and fired twice. Rohan dropped dead on the table with his eyes wide open. He and Jax stared at each for a second before he stood. Jax, that is because Rohan would stand no more. Not in this life. The man spun on his heels and rushed back out of the restaurant. The patrons didn't see him on the way out either since they'd ducked from the gun shots and took cover.

"I gotta bounce," Jax said and stood. He grabbed the beer bottle with his prints and DNA and calmly walked out the back.

****

"That must be Little Wop," Reese said in reply to the knock at her door. They were both dressed in less to impress but needed some more drugs for the night. Reese cuffed the rest of hers so Michelle could spend some of that good suburban housewife money.

"Wow! You look just like your father!" Michelle exclaimed when the young dealer walked in. In a twist of twisted hood irony his lookalike dad had once delivered drugs to these same two once upon a time. Big Wop was now upstate waiting on his son to join him.

"Err body say that," the young man said, flashing the exact same smile that allowed his old man to bed them both back in the day. In yet another ironic twist Reese had sucked his dick one late night for drugs just like she had his dad's.

"Damn! You know what, let me get another one to take home!" Michelle said seeing the pretty eight ball in her hand. Little Wop gladly produced another, adding the additional cash to his growing bank roll. He was heading out to a club too and the extra bread meant extra flossing. Just like his father, he tricked off his money as fast as he earned it.

"A'ight yo. Hit me up if you need something else," he said as he made his way out of the apartment.

"So, let's hit The Palace! That shit be jumping!" Reese cheered and winded her hips to the music playing. The short skirt threatened to give up some of the pretty black ass cheeks it barely concealed. Michelle too wore a tiny dress to show off her thick thighs and round ass.

"Nah, that shit too wild. Let's hit somewhere low key with rich men sipping expensive liquor." she suggested. "I just wanna chill and get tipsy. I ain't tryna fight or dodge no damn bullets!"

"You talking my language now. I know just the place. I'll call us a taxi," she said like old times.

"Taxi! Bitch, I'm pushing something new. Fuck I look like catching a gypsy cab!" she shot back since it wasn't old times. They each snorted one more line off the coffee table then hit the door.

Megan had been in the window watching the show since the malt liquor had retired her grandmother to bed. It had been entertaining to say the least as she watched the ebb and flow of drug traffic as well as a couple of teens making out hot and heavy on a bench. They slid inside one of the buildings to finish what they'd started in a stairwell. She dipped back behind the curtain when she heard her mother's laughter. Slowly she leaned back so she could see but not be seen. Her eyes went wide when she saw her mother and friend stagger, laughing and loud talking through the court yard. They went even wider when she saw what she was wearing. She remembered her parents fussing about clothes just like the ones she had on now.

Michelle sensed her daughter staring at her from the window just like her own mom did back in the days when she'd marched through without even looking up. Megan let out a lonely sigh when it was obvious she wasn't coming to get her. Her grandmother had beat her out of all her allowance before passing out from drinking two forties. She wanted to call her dad but remembered her mother's warning. Luckily there would be plenty to see out the project window. The night was still young and grandma didn't have cable or internet.

****

"Where is this place?" Michelle fussed and shimmied in the driver's seat from needing to pee.

"Down in the village, oh I mean Chelsea. You know they changed the whole name when the Clinton's moved down there," Reese said. "This the spot though. Nothing but ballers! Black, white, Spanish and Chinese. All spending dough."

She didn't let on that it was a good place to turn a discreet trick for some extra cash. Most of the patrons were wealthy business men looking for some strange before going home to the norm. Tricks or no tricks it was still a swank little place to hang out. Mellow jazz and a blind eye to drug use.

"Uh oh. Looks like someone got hurt," Michelle announced as they drove passed a crime scene. Nosey drivers slowed to a crawl to watch police activity at a corner pizza parlor.

"Killed, look," Reese said as medical examiner clerks brought out a body bag.

"Dang!" Michelle said. She had no way of knowing it was her husband who was zipped up inside. She would find out soon enough but now it was time to get her party on.

Chapter 10

"Look who's here," XL said as Jax entered Back Shots. To both their surprise he made a beeline towards them without stopping to gawk, grope or flirt with any of the naked women. It was still his mission to dip his dick in each and every one of them but it would have to wait. First things first because he had some cocaine to buy.

"With a bag full of cash, I see," Snake said acknowledging the satchel in his hand and extra pep in his step. The heavy swing of the bag indicated it weighed a couple hundred grand. "And I still ain't fucking with him until he handles that business."

"Or gets handled," the body guard added as they had been discussing. Jax was a loose end that needed to either be tied up or cut off. He would either kill or be killed. It was he who'd brought the cop into the club and that shit wasn't going to float.

"Three-hundred-grand. I'll be through in the morning to pick up my work." he said thrusting the bag of cash to the help. XL looked to his boss who gave the nod to accepted the cash.

"Has the deed been done?" Snake asked even though he was pretty sure it had been. Dude was cocky, reckless even but not crazy. Actually, he was crazy but he wasn't stupid.

"Watch the news," he replied over his shoulder as he turned to leave. He spotted the girl from the funeral on his way out and mentally moved her to the top of his list. She must have told Rohan about his sister leaving with XL. That was a problem and she probably had to die. He was still going to fuck her first though.

First things first since he'd just received word that his partner was killed, so he had to head downtown to join his comrades.

****

"Girl, where's the bathroom?" Michelle demanded once they were inside. She spotted the sign as Reese pointed towards it and took off.

"Yeah, that way!" Reese laughed at her dilemma and found a booth. Reese rushed over and slid into one that a couple had just vacated. She could tell from the look in their faces and bulge in his slacks that they wouldn't be coming back. Young thots and rich married men made this hookup central.

The unisex symbol above the door didn't register until she rushed by a man standing in front of a urinal. She thought she was in the wrong place until a woman came out of a stall with relief written all over her face. Michelle rushed into the abandoned stall for relief of her own.

"Whew!" she exclaimed over the loud stream of urine. Luckily for her she was barely dressed and didn't have much clothing to slow her up. The borrowed dress was so short she didn't even have to lift it to sit down. She pulled the thin strip of thong out the way and let go. Not that it was enough to cover the fat mound of vagina she was blessed with. The coke in her purse suggested she take a quick bump once her bladder was empty. She complied and took two scoops like a Raisin Bran commercial.

Once the flow stopped she patted her pussy dry with a napkin from her purse and stood. She stepped back out into the club and looked around for her friend. She spotted her waving hand and made her way over through the crowd of handsome men. Men who smiled, nodded or lifted their glass to her instead of the gropes and "Sup yo", she would have gotten in some hood club.

"You straight now?" Reese giggled while motioning for her to wipe the cocaine residue from her nose.

"My bad," she apologized as if she owed one. "You wanna go take a bump?"

"Shit, I can get straight right here," she said accepting the drugs. She worked under the table using an airbrushed finger nail to shovel the drugs into her nostrils.

"Damn, you were right! There's some ballers in here," Michelle said, smiling back at an investment banker type smiling at her from the bar. All the men in here were wearing tailored suits or a casual equivalent. Their wealth in stocks, bonds and real estate rather than hanging from their neck or parked out back.

"Yeah, but I got one question. Why come every time a black man start getting money he shave his mustache?" Reese wondered. "That's some creepy shit! Look like they'll suck your pussy inside out!"

"That's a good question. I'm 'bout to ask him," Michelle laughed as the man from the bar approached. Her returning his smile obviously translated to an invitation.

"Ladies," he greeted, parting his thick lips into an expensive smile. Both stifled a giggle at the bare chunk of meat between his nose and lips. Both spotted the place where he removed his wedding ring. Neither cared.

"Hey!" they both sang, like they did as teens when grown men pushed up on them.

"Can I buy you, ladies, a drink?" he offered, raising a hand to summon the waitress.

"Champagne, thank you," Reese accepted before Michelle could decline. He slid in next to Michelle indicating his preference and ordered a bottle.

"Gregory Jackson," he said extending his large hand. Michelle giggled at the attention and shook his strong hand and inhaled his strong cologne. It was as intoxicating as any of the intoxicants already in her system.

"I'm Michelle," she admitted instead of her usual club name, Shantay. Shantay had quite a rep for fucking on first dates back in the day. Not that Michelle's reputation was much better around the way.

"I'm Reese," Reese tossed across the table even though it was obvious he only had eyes for her friend. She watched as Michelle giggled coyly to his conversation.

A man at the bar raised his glass in greeting when Reese looked in his direction. She squinted through the dimness of the club and drug fogged memory trying to place the face. She couldn't so she decided to investigate.

"Excuse me," she said only because she knew her friend and her new friend weren't paying her any attention and wouldn't miss her. The man at the bar smile widened with every step she took towards him.

"Reese, right? Grand Marnier, right?" he said recalling both her name and drink.

"But of course," she giggled and struggled to remember him. He was too familiar to just have exchanged numbers but nothing more came to mind. They engaged in small talk while she waited for some clue to jog her memory.

****

"Jax is here," a cop informed when he arrived at the still active murder scene. An additional wave of grief swept through the grim scene as the cop who lost his partner arrived.

"What the fuck?" Jax asked with a pained expression as he entered the pizza parlor for the second time that day. He was slightly relieved the body had been removed already because it was some fuck shit. Necessary fuck shit, but fuck shit none the less.

"I'm sorry," a fellow officer offered. He would have been able to feel his pain since he'd lost a partner a few months back. Not quite the same since he didn't have him killed like

Jax had. It was open season on cops since cops declared open season on blacks. The whole, 'rabbits got the gun' and no, they didn't find it fun either.

"Surveillance? Does this dump have cameras?" he asked looking around knowing they didn't. "Witnesses? Don't tell me no one saw nothing!"

"There were a few people inside when it happened. Guy in hoodie walks in, pops him and walks out. We got a couple people downtown but they ducked when the shooting started."

"I see," Jax sighed giving himself a mental pat on the back at the perfect crime. It was a sign of his own cocky naivety because there is no such thing as a perfect crime.

Cops and CSI techs milled about looking for needles in haystacks. The seasoned detectives knew this was a hit and didn't expect to find any clues here. They went through the motions and played along knowing the crime scene had nothing to do with the crime. They would do better checking Rohan's phone records and bank accounts. If he had a mistress or gambling habits. This wasn't about the pizza.

"Has any one told his wife?" the captain asked shaking his head. If not, he would have to do it and he hated that part of the job. A duty he had to discharge more and more often during cop season. He would probably do better telling his cops to stop gunning down unarmed black men.

"I'll do it. I know Michelle pretty good," Jax offered. The captain nodded in agreement then rushed off to the coroner's office.

****

"What we got?" Captain asked as he entered the morgue. The smell of death mingled with the stainless steel and embalming fluid creating a uniquely pungent aroma that clings to clothing and skin. It even gets stuck in nostrils like a whiff of pure bleach.

"Dead cop," the M.E said stoically since there was a dead cop laying naked on the slab in front of them. "Two small caliber rounds, .380 most likely, I haven't removed them yet."

"I see," the superior said, twisting his lips as he looked at where the medical examiner shaved around the bullets holes. He couldn't help but notice they looked like eyes. "Too bad he didn't have eyes in the back of his head or he would have saw this coming."

"Yeah," the doctor replied because what else was there to say to that. "His phone, keys and weapon are in the bag."

"OK. I'll send the detectives assigned to the case to collect them." the captain said. He let out one more sigh and shook his head once more before crossing his Catholic heart and rushing from the room.

****

"So, same price? Same thing?" the unnamed stranger finally asked as they reached the bottom of their third drink. The small talk still hadn't refreshed her cloudy memory.

"What?" Reese asked hoping whatever that thing was might ring a bell.

"Well, last time we met we went to my place. A grand for a trip around the world," he reminded. Poor fellow didn't know Reese gave trips around the projects for a lot less. She once fucked in the stairwell for six wings, some fries and a dime bag.

"Oh Yeah! Now, I remember you!" she shouted as it came rushing back. She remembered he'd sucked and fucked her so well he'd almost gotten some of his money back. "Hell yeah! Let's ride!"

"Don't you have to tell your friend you're leaving?" the man asked as they walked arm in arm towards the door.

"Who?" she asked looking in the direction he nodded in. She saw Michelle and Greg snuggled up close getting along great. A grand in the hand beats a bird in the bush so she shook her head and kept moving. "She good."

"I know this chick...Wow, Reese," Michelle said, seeing her friend flee the club. It wasn't the first time she'd left her in some club for some dick. If she had a dime for every time she left her she'd have quite a few dimes

"Was that your ride? I can take you home. Your home, my home?" he asked hopefully. He reached his hand under her tiny dress to explain what he was after.

"Ssss, I'm married," she hissed, sounding disappointed at the revelation. She of course didn't know yet that she was a widow. She still didn't stop him from pawing her pussy though. In fact, she did the opposite and parted her thighs a little so he could get to it better.

"Shit!" Greg fussed when she soaked his whole hand down to the wrist. His mind instantly processed every word he knew or heard looking for the combination that would get his dick inside this juicy box. The thought crossed his mind to lean down and suck a mouthful of that sweet nectar. Instead he kept working his thick finger in and out of her slippery pussy.

"Man, this-s-s...is...Ssss...fucked up," she complained when she felt an orgasm creeping up on her. She knew fighting it was not only futile but would only make her come that much harder. Instead she leaned over and took his tongue down her throat to muffle her screaming orgasm.

"I only have eight hundred dollars on me," he pleaded horse from desire. A waste of money since she'd just made up her mind to fuck him. It was Rohan's fault she was here so she shrugged and stood with him.

"Where are we going?" she asked as they rushed towards the exit. She hoped it was close before she came to her senses and changed her mind. Plus, it was obvious he was married. Takes one to know one since she was married too.

"I keep an apartment nearby in the city," he explained without explaining he lived out in Jersey with his wife and children. To ease the killer commute, he kept a studio in the city where he worked. To ease the loneliness, he bought some pussy from time to time from the bar.

"OK," she said as he opened the door of a new Benz so she could sit. She looked over to the crime scene still bustling with cops even though it was moot. Greg reached over to fondle her vagina to keep it wet and hot as he bent corners to his apartment.

"Evening, Mr. Jackson," the doorman greeted as he pulled to a stop out front. He tossed him the keys in reply and rushed her inside.

"Nice," Michelle complimented as they entered the unit. Those were her last words before he stuck his tongue back in her mouth.

They fell on the plush futon and feverishly undressed each other. Michelle wanted to clap for him when a nice thick dick emerged from his bikini underwear. It was so thick and hard she excused his bikini underwear. She noticed her own wedding rings and bands as she gripped the cock in her left hand. Guilt made her switch hands but didn't stop her from leaning in and taking him into her mouth.

It was Rohan's fault that she sucked and stroked his dick while he played in her pussy. Blame him that she came all over his fingers again. It was her fault for swallowing a torrent of semen when he exploded in her mouth.

"Argh! Mmm. Whew!" Greg fussed as he spasms from an orgasm and filled her mouth. That was just the appetizer like a plate of mushroom caps stuffed with cheese. They stood so he could let out the futon so he could stuff her with dick.

Again, she wanted to clap seeing his dick was just as hard. She was glad he got that first nut out the way so they could fuck. And fuck they did.

"No, flip over," he ordered as she attempted to lay on her back. She smiled wickedly over her shoulder as she complied.

"Like this?" she asked with a playful pout and arched her back. Her fat vagina poked out like a Jack in the box.

"Just like that," he agreed and climbed on. He took a second to run his fat mushroom shaped head in the froth between her swollen labia. She wiggled her ass from side to in anticipation. He eased inside and let his body weight sink him slowly, deep inside.

"Can't go no further," she warned when he nestled against her cervix. She said he could have some pussy, not ovaries or fallopian tubes.

He replied by slowly backing out to the hilt and plunging back to the bottom. She saw where this was going and gripped handfuls of the sheets to brace herself for a pounding. Men are just as rough on rental pussy as they are with rental cars. He mercilessly beat on it since he kept his main one safe and sound at home.

Michelle had orgasm after orgasm as he dug her out. It reminded her of the rough sex with rough necks growing up in the Bronx. Before getting married to a gentleman who made gentle love to her. Likewise, the gentleman inside of her at the moment didn't, couldn't fuck his fancy wife in this manner either.

"Turn over!" he said urgently and snatched himself free for her snatch. He flipped her onto her back so he could fuck her face to face as the end drew near.

Michelle pulled her legs far and wide by the back of her knees, giving herself up completely. He took it all too by slamming against her cervix with each long, hard thrust.

"Shit!" Greg cursed as he pulled out and came on her stomach. Now she had his seed both in and on her belly. "Can you stay longer or, you have to go?"

"Can I use your bathroom?" she replied, opting to stay. That meant she needed to powder her nose with powdered cocaine to fuel round two, three and whatever was to come. After all, this was all her husband's fault.

Chapter 11

I'll never forget the feeling I had when I woke up that day. I felt an emptiness as if a piece of my soul had been stolen. In retrospect, I guess I could feel not feeling his presence anymore. A part of me died that day too.

"Good morning, sweetie. You hungry?" Megan's grandmother sang cheerfully as her groggy grandchild staggered into the front room. She knew her little nosey ass had been up all night looking out the window. Megan told herself she was just waiting on her mother to return but the sights she saw pushed her to the back of her mind.

She had a birds-eye view when Mookie confronted Black about stealing his pack. Whatever that meant, led to a fist fight that Black got the best of. Mookie wasn't prepared to lose his pack and get his ass whooped all in the same night. He produced a small pistol and pointed it at Black. Black dared him to shoot while hurling curses that made the sheltered child blush. Being called a 'fuck nigga' was the straw that pulled the trigger.

Oddly Megan wasn't scared by the act of violence she witnessed. If anything, it intrigued her. She watched curiously as paramedics loaded the injured man on a gurney and took him away. Even more fascinating was that Mookie was in the crowd of spectators watching the after show after the shooting. Police even asked him if he saw what happened as they nonchalantly processed the shooting. They knew no one saw nothing and just went through the motions. Much to her surprise even Black claimed not to see who shot him.

"Baby?" Dianne asked when the girl didn't reply. The events of the previous night pulled her to the window so she could see what she could see. A quick scan of the parking lot showed that her mother hadn't returned from her night on the town even though it was morning.

"Yes, Grandmother?" she replied as if she just noticed her presence.

"I said, are you hungry?" she repeated and headed to the kitchen to cook regardless of her reply.

"Yes," Megan replied while her head shook 'no'. She was still leery about eating anything from the roach infested kitchen but she was starving and had no idea when her mother would return.

The woman began to pull out all the fixings for a continental breakfast knowing her daughter would be hung over whenever she came in. Nothing soaks up alcohol and neutralizes cocaine like steak, cheese eggs, biscuits and hash browns. Meanwhile, Megan posted back up in the window and went back to people watching. She amused herself even more by imitating the colorful inhabitants.

"Sup yo?" she repeated and pretended to give a pound and man hug like the two men who greeted below. They were cool but she was delighted when the group of preteen girls came back out. They obviously didn't get much more sleep than she did since they'd dispersed in the wee hours of the morning and were now right back on their bench to make sure they didn't miss anything.

"I heard Black got shot last night!" one said setting off a round of gossip. Megan gleamed that she was the leader of the young ratchets since she took center stage and dictated the flow of conversation. That's why Megan copied her every word and gesture.

"Mommy," Megan cheered to herself when she saw her mother's truck pull in. She hoped they could leave and go back to their comfortable life in their comfortable home. "Grandmother, my mommy's back."

"She right on time," she called back and began to fix the plates. She knew her daughter well enough to know she would be hungry and hung over after a night on the town. Back in the day she would need an ice pack for her beat up box.

"Sorry, we can't stay for breakfast grandmother," Megan offered apologetically and began to prepare to leave.

"Ok, baby," Dianne chuckled since she knew better. Knew that her child was about to stumble in, smash and crash.

"Whew!" Michelle giggled to herself as she stepped from the truck and wobbled. Her swollen vagina throbbed below so it was probably good that she'd left her thong behind with her dignity. The bare lipped stranger had fucked her every which way but loose. He got his eight hundred dollars' worth out of her but it was still Rohan's fault have her tell it.

Megan watched with a curious frown as her mother staggered towards the building. It was the same stagger Reese had hours earlier when she'd returned from her own episode.

Bad Cop

They both got thoroughly dicked down along with drugs and alcohol.

"Sup yo?" Michelle greeted. Her voice was strained and horse from several screaming orgasms. She had yelled, 'that's it', 'right there', fuck me', and 'I'm coming' all night and into the morning.

"I'm ready!" Megan sang trying to steer her back out the door. She had all her little belongings ready to bounce.

"You cooked, Ma?" she asked, ignoring her child in favor of the aroma wafting in the air. She was eager to get something in her stomach besides all the cum she'd swallowed.

"Sure did," she replied, sitting the plates on the small dinette table. "Come on and eat, baby."

"OK," Megan groaned in defeat. She tried to pretend like she didn't see any roaches crawling around so she could fill her empty stomach.

Megan had never seen her mother fresh from a hangover and stared oddly as she stuffed her face. The only sounds to be heard was metal forks hitting the old school plates as they ate.

"'Bout to lay down for a minute," Michelle announced once her plate was empty. She stood, wobbled and entered the freezer. Her mother shook her head as Michelle fixed an ice pack.

"Can we go home now?" Megan asked hopefully. "Daddy is going to be worried."

"He'll be a'ight, and don't you call him!" she insisted and wobbled away. Michelle rolled along the hallway wall and

104

into her old room. It was just like old times when she'd crash out after a night of sex, drugs and drinking. Just like old times it would be afternoon when she finally got back up again.

"You wanna try to win your money back?" Dianne asked with a sly giggle. The poor girl was a lot poorer since her grandmother made up the rules as she went along.

"No thank you, Grandmother," she sighed and went back to her perch in the window.

****

"Just nosey," Michelle laughed when she found her daughter in the window hours later when she awoke.

"Can we go home now?" she asked once more. Twenty-four hours in the hood was plenty and she was ready to go home to the burbs.

"Yeah, we are going home," she said sending the girl scrambling for her shoes. "We out, Ma."

"OK, baby, what's this for?" Dianne asked as her daughter extended a roll of cash towards her. She always acted surprised when her daughter broke her off some bread.

"You," she replied coming off a couple of the eight hundred dollars from her night on the town. Why not since she fucked the man for free and he paid her. She gave her mom a hug and turned for the door.

"Bye, Grandmother," Megan called out happily as they departed. Leaving was always better than coming so it was genuine.

Michelle started to call her husband when she reached her truck. She looked at his contact, scrunched her face, shook her head and changed her mind. Megan craned her neck out the window to get a last look at the ghetto as they departed. She saw the leader of the young ratchets coming from the bodega and waved. After watching and imitating her all night she mentally befriended the girl. In her mind, she was part of her little crew from the bench. The girl shot her a bird and rolled her eyes before ducking into her building.

Michelle lifted her chin to spite the guilt that was eating at her. Her vagina throbbed below as a reminder of the night of rough sex. Rohan was going to have to settle for a good blow job after their argument. She planned to play victim, make him feel guilty then suck his dick in forgiveness. Probably would have worked if he wasn't laying on a slab in the morgue.

"Wake up, Megan," she said, frowning at the car parked in front of her house. She watched it cautiously as she pulled into her driveway and parked. She reached for the pistol her husband made her keep in her purse when the car door began to open.

"That's daddy's friend," Megan announced, recognizing Jax before her mother did. That's because she hadn't drank, did drugs and stayed up all night.

"Go in the house," she urged as Jax approached. The look on his face foretold the grim news to come. Her husband's car wasn't here but his partner was and that could only mean one thing. Both Michelle and Jax waited and watched as the chubby girl climbed the steps. She worked the keys in the lock, opened the door and cast a glance behind before stepping inside. "Is my husband dead?"

"It was quick. Painless even," he said nodding his head solemnly. An excellent show of contrition; especially since he was involved in the murder.

"Oh no!" she wailed as her knees buckled below. Luckily Jax was close enough to catch her before she went down.

"I know, I know," he comforted and held her tightly to himself. She moaned and wailed deep, heartfelt sobs at the devastating news. Fucking and sucking all night added to her grief. Jax fought against the erection throbbing to life but she felt so soft and smelled so good. He lost that fight and a hard dick soon stood between them. Michelle pulled her face back to look at him but left her body pressed against him. "My bad. I..."

"What's wrong, Mommy?" Megan wanting to know as she came back out. She had been watching from the window and saw the near collapse.

"Go back inside! I'll be there in a minute," she said finally backing away from the dick. Even in her moment of grief she cast quick glance at the bulge in his pants.

"Um, let me know if you need any help with anything. Of course, the city will handle arrangements. I guess you can inform his mom?" he asked.

"No." she said. The hateful old lady wouldn't even know her son was gone if it was up to her.

"Well, I'll do the notification. Call if you need, any...thing," he said in a manner to include his dick too. She accepted his card and turned to walk into the house. Jax watched her shapely ass until it disappeared inside. He turned to go notify Rohan's mother since it was on the way to Back Shots.

"What's wrong, Mommy!" Megan shouted when her mother walked in. She stomped her foot and put a hand on her hip just like her mother did when she was mad.

"Bitch, who you talking to? Huh, bitch?" Michelle snapped. She closed the distance between them in a flash and began to beat the girl. Pummel as if she was back in the projects fighting her fellow hood rats.

Megan took the first few blows dead on since she was in shock. Instinct finally kicked in and told her ball up to deflect the blows. A lesson she would need later in life. Her arms and back burned from the punches and finally kicks being hurled at her. The expletives being sent her way hurt even more.

"Fat ass, little bitch. Questioning me like you my damn mother! My husband dead and you trying to run shit!" she fussed as she fought her child.

Megan's body bounced to the beating but she no longer felt it. The pain of hearing that her father was gone turned her body numb.

Michelle ran out of steam and collapsed next to her child. They both sat and sobbed as the next chapter of their lives was being written.

Chapter 12

"Bullshit," Jax sighed as he parked in the project parking lot. His new car made the young thugs eyes go wide with larceny. He pulled his badge hanging on a chain from under his shirt and got out. A corner of his shirt rode up showing the handle of one of the three guns he carried.

"Five-O," one of the teens announced and they all spread out to give him space.

"Keep an eye on my shit for me," he said tossing one a bag of weed.

"Ain't nobody gone fuck with it!" the recipient of the fluffy buds vowed. Jax nodded and memorized their faces just in case. He checked the address again and headed towards the building to handle the death notification.

"Yes?" Maria asked as she opened the door without asking who first. A sign she was as reckless and naive as her dead mother. She recognized the man from the funeral before he even spoke. "Hello?"

"Is your grandmother home?" he asked alternating his gaze between her pretty hazel eyes and little breast nubs on her shirt. The same ones that made her stick her chest out to show off her introduction to puberty.

"Yes," she replied just as her grandmother came from the back.

"Who is it?" Mrs. Mahatma called from the hallway knowing her dimwitted grandchild would open the door for anyone.

"Mrs. Robinson, I'm um... Detective Jax, Ja-Jackson. I was your son's partner," he began. The old woman frowned at the usage of past tense and tensed.

"It's Mahatma. What's going on?" she asked him and turned to Maria. "Call your uncle!"

"Would it be OK if we spoke alone?" he asked so they child would leave. Maria left on her own while dialing her uncle's number. Jax squinted at her back side but there wasn't much to see yet. "I regret to inform you that..."

"No!" the woman shouted and took off down the hall as if not hearing it wouldn't make it true. Losing one child is too much, but two is beyond any parents' ability. A moment later Maria returned wearing a scowl.

"What you do to her?" the little girl demanded, putting hands on hips she didn't yet have.

"Told her, her son passed away. Here, tell her to call me," he said giving the shocked child his business card. As far as he was concerned he made the death notifications so he was done. He turned to leave because he had to head across town where he had enough bricks to build a house.

Maria rushed to the back to verify the news and got it when she found her grandmother broken into a heap on her bed. She felt tears warming her face as she climbed in to join her.

****

Jax felt himself stiffen when he saw the sign for Back Shots ahead of him. It wasn't the sexy woman on the billboard or any of the morally challenged women who worked there that got him excited. It was all that coke he was going to pick up. His squad of hungry dope slinging hyenas were ready to push his product. They didn't mind busting their guns either as Pop had proved by putting his partner in the obituary columns.

Jax parked near the same back door Pocahontas was escorted out of when XL lead her off to slaughter. He ditty bopped around front and made his way through the club. It was late afternoon but the place was already bustling. The women who worked days usually had husbands and children at home and were just looking to earn a few extra bucks. When they left the crew of students and professional hoes came to shake and rent their asses.

The club actually had a really good lunch menu to attract businessmen to come eat, drink and sometimes turn a quick trick. The radio played at a moderate level instead of a DJ blaring the latest strip music.

Jax poked his bottom lip out and nodded approvingly at the day shift as he made his way through the club. There were a couple of women he decided to put on his hit list and hit. He bypassed the VIP section and headed to the management office.

"Yeah," XL barked as he snatched open the door. He scowled at Jax before stepping aside to let him in.

"Sup yo?" Jax greeted graciously. He gave the bodyguard a pound and hug despite reaffirming his plan to murder him first chance he got. He smiled in delight at the neat pile of bricks on Snake's desk. "My nigga!"

"I bet I am," Snake laughed at his reaction. He knew Jax would make more off the cocaine than he did. That's why he decided to press him for a percentage when the time was right. He knew that it was too soon in the relationship to ask for extras, just like men know to wait a couple of dates before asking for head.

"This shit is beautiful!" he exclaimed as he examined a kilo. It was so potent he could smell it straight through the wrapper. "I'll be done in a couple of days or so and be ready for more."

"Come on with it! Oh, and I saw your handiwork on the news," he said smiling over the constant coverage of the dead cop on every channel. He had to admire the fact that there was no surveillance and no witnesses.

"Yeah," he replied with a smile and nod since he planned to put him on the news too. As soon as he figured out who this middleman was in the middle of his ass was dead too.

"Come celebrate with me tonight," Snake offered, throwing in free drinks and vagina.

"How can I say no?" he laughed, nodded and accepted. Pounds were pounded and Jax set off with his work. He loaded it in a duffle bag and hoisted it on his shoulder.

****

"You staying here!" Michelle barked as she stuck her head into her daughter's room. She didn't look at her because she didn't want to see or accept all the bumps and bruises she'd left behind. The sudden rage scared them both but left her embarrassed as well.

"OK," she replied without looking either, for the same reason. She could still hear the slaps and 'bitches' echoing in her mind hours later. There were deep welts on her arms from trying to block the blows. The inside of her lip felt like it was shredded from the beating. No, she didn't want to go anywhere with the woman.

Michelle had the grim task of signing for her husband's body so he could be buried. Luckily, he was a police officer and already formally identified or she'd have had to do that too. She felt pretty lucky when she found the extra eight ball she purchased the night before. It was just what the doctor ordered. She'd sipped and snorted until it was time to go.

Megan jumped online as soon as she heard her mother leave the house. Her first destination was to research child abuse laws. She didn't plan on taking the ass whipping for free. Michelle was going to jail for that one. She was sidetracked by the local news on her homepage. She just knew the murdered cop on her screen was her father. She clicked and read about his case.

Meanwhile, Michelle was so high from cocaine and cognac that she blasted the music and danced in her seat as she rode back into the city. Her mind was a million miles away from all the troubles in her life. Two million from all the trouble headed full steam ahead into her life.

An hour later she pulled up at the medical examiner's office and parked. She reached in her purse to take a hit but a glance around returned too many glances back. The place was jumping with activity in a city with such a high murder rate. The morgue wasn't the latest club or hot spot but people were dying to get in.

"Shit!" Michelle fussed more from not being able to get a one on one up each nostril than being at the morgue. Until she remembered why she was there then cursed again. "Shit!"

The captain was expecting her and jumped to his feet when she entered the building. He'd met her on several occasions over the years but still asked one of his trademark silly questions.

"Mrs. Robinson?" he asked earning his nickname of Captain Obvious.

"Yes," she fussed knowing he knew. "What happened to my husband?"

"We're not sure just yet. He was working undercover in narcotics and may have been discovered? It could be retaliation from someone he put in jail already? We just don't know but, rest assured someone will pay!"

"So, what about us? His family, are we in danger? How are we supposed to take care of ourselves?" she asked desperately as the desperation of her situation set in. It coincided with her high crashing down as well. A couple scoops of powder would have cheered her right up, right then.

"Well, I doubt anyone knows where you live but I can ask Suffolk county police to keep an eye out. As for the family, his insurance and pension will take good care of you," he gently assured. "You need to come downtown on Monday to sign the insurance claim."

"Oh yeah!" she cheered a little too cheerfully for the occasion. This was the morgue after all and her husband was down the hall stretched out. She had married the man for his steady income and never thought much about the insurance policies he kept. Her mind went to the small lock box he kept them along with their other important documents in. "Can I see him?"

"I, um...guess. I'll tell the M.E," the captain said and rushed off to do just that.

Meanwhile, Michelle thought about the hundreds of thousands she had coming her way. Rohan would be able to support his family in death just as he did in life. Nothing would change except her husband was never coming home again. That sent genuine tears pouring from her eyes. She had all but changed her mind about seeing him when the captain came back.

"Follow me," he instructed so she followed him. He led the way around a few corners and stopped in front of a window with a drawn curtain. He looked down from his six feet four-inch vantage point raising his brow in question. She nodded a tentative 'yes' so he tapped on the glass.

"Oh, Rohan!" she groaned when the curtain separated and she saw her husband separated from his soul. Some dead people look like they're sleeping peacefully but not Rohan. He had a perturbed look on his face as if to say, *this is some real bullshit*. Little did he know the real bullshit was yet to come.

"That's enough," captain said tapping on the glance once more. The man inside quickly closed them and put Rohan back in his drawer. The funeral home could now claim him since his wife had signed for him.

"Where's the bathroom?" Michelle croaked through the grief in her throat. She nodded her thanks when he pointed her in the right direction. He felt slightly guilty looking at her ass as she rushed away since her dead husband lay just behind the curtain. Still, it was a nice round ass so he looked until she ducked into the bathroom.

Michelle was barely inside the stall when she rambled through her purse and dug out the blow. A huge scoop up each nostril provided instant relief for the antsy feeling that overcame her when her high wore off. The depression eased and a smile spread on her face. She put the drugs away and high stepped from the stall.

"Hey now," she giggled at her reflection. She wiped the cocaine residue from her nose and shook her head. It was time to go home and dig out the insurance policies.

Chapter 13

"Lookie, lookie!" Jax proclaimed as he entered upon his Brooklyn crew in his Brooklyn stash house. All eyes went wide when he produced five of the kilos he'd just purchased. He decided to keep the rest at home. What better place to stash them since he was a cop.

"Yo!" Pop cheered at the riches before them. He felt like his stock had risen since he'd put in some work.

"Well, let's get to cooking," Mano announced and paused the video game. He was the strictly business member of the crew while the others were more on the wild side. He was slightly in his feelings about Pop getting the call to pop the cop. Dude was running his mouth about it already. Just among the crew, but as soon as he got some pussy he would tell her during pillow talk. Then talk tough in the barbershop to whoever was listening.

The men stood and headed into the kitchen. It was more lab than kitchen despite having two complete stoves in it. Only takeout was eaten here because this was strictly for cooking dope. Jax was the first to don a mask even before the packages were bust open. He kept a high level of cocaine in his system at all times but crack fumes are a different animal. Tyrannosaurus actually, and who needs that in their life.

"Bruh, this shit is raw doggie!" Larry said getting a whiff of the drugs before donning his own mask. Jax was elated at the 100% raw dope, but kept a poker face.

The men worked in silence save the Erv-G CD playing in the system. Heads bobbed to the funky tracks as powder was turned into rocks. Hours later a mountain range of cocaine lay on the table drying. Once it was dry it would be weighed again to see what it ended up as. Each man's batch was kept separate so they could earn bragging rights on who had the meanest whip game.

"Yo, you seen that shit on the news about that cop?" Pop asked once more. He'd already bragged to Mano but now the rest of the crew was present.

"Chill B," Jax warned while Mano shot him an *I told you so* with twisted lips and raised brows. Jax gave half a nod in acquiescence since he did indeed tell him so. Not that Jax didn't already know his man had loose lips. Question was, would he be allowed to sink his ship.

"Oh yeah!" Pop said looking at his partners as if they were the ones who couldn't hold water. None of them were tuned in so missed the brief exchange.

"Moment of truth," Mano announced when he checked the dope and saw it was dry. "I got a band say mines at least doubled!"

"Shit I got a band for whoever got the best whip," Jax offered. A little bonus for his employees like a good employer. There would be another bonus for whoever moved theirs the quickest.

The banter increased as they all weighed up their products. In the end, it was Mano who came out on top. Pop took second place and got a reward as well. Jax pulled him aside to whisper just like when he gave the order for the hit.

"Yo, we hitting the club tonight. Don't say shit to them or they gonna wanna come too," he challenged the man.

"That's what's up," he smiled and nodded. He wanted to be the man next to the man but Mano held that position, until now that is since Jax asked him to hang out with him. He pressed his index finger to his lips indicating he could and would keep the secret. He couldn't and wouldn't and was going to brag far and wide first thing in the morning.

"You got rid of that hammer, right?" he asked since it was part of the initial order.

"Huh?" he asked meaning *no*. He liked the brand-new plastic pistol so much he wanted to hang on to it. Despite it having a cop's body on it. Guns with bodies on them are bad but cop bodies, are the worse.

"Bring it tonight. I'll see you in a few," Jax whispered before turning back to the rest and raising his voice. "Yo, five percent extra if you done in 24 hours."

The raise got a cheer and fist pumps as the men set out to get money. The extra percent would allow them to make deals and sales to move the dope quicker and still make money.

"Well, let's hit the street and get rich," Mano said sending everyone in motion.

"Yeah!" Pop cheered and shot Jax a wink at their little secret. Instead of hitting the block he went home to change. Jax did the same and they met back up for a night on the town.

****

"The Bronx?" Pop asked cautiously as they entered the notorious borough. He was a local joker who rarely ventured far from his hood let alone to other parts of the city. His universe was no bigger than his section of Brooklyn.

"Yeah, we 'bout to hit Back Shots. They got the baddest bitches in the city," Jax replied sounding just like the commercial.

"They don't be fucking," he dared, cocking his head dubiously, although hoping with all he had that they were fucking.

"Who? Bruh, I bang a different broad err night out that joint!" he said truthfully. He spelled out his exploits for the rest of the ride out to the club.

"Wow!" the young thug exclaimed once they were inside. He whipped his head to and fro trying to take it all in. He'd never seen anything but neighborhood young black thots naked, in person so the ethnic breast and bare vaginas amazed him.

Jax was just as pleased when he spotted the woman from the funeral on a side stage twerking for twenties. He glanced over to the VIP and saw both Snake and his help staring back. He gave half a nod and escorted his own help to a table.

"Sup boss?" XL asked in confusion. His low IQ kept him in a constant haze of confusion, constantly having to have things explained to him.

"Nothing. He good," Snake replied. He and Jax spoke earlier so he knew tonight was Diamond's last night working. Doing anything for that matter since it was her last night on earth. That's why she was dancing with a belly full of his semen now. He had her in his office earlier for a going away blow job.

"Wow!" Pop said again and again as he saw women from all over the globe. He clapped for the Asian waitress when she delivered a bottle of champagne. It was his going away party and he didn't even know it.

"Yo, send Diamond over when she gets off stage," Jax told the woman. She nodded, like a geisha girl despite actually being from Harlem, and tipped away with her tip.

"Them Chinese bitches' pussy sideways," Pop advised nodding as if it was fact, not some dumb ass fiction.

"Yup," Jax agreed since it didn't matter. He toasted with him and scanned the club for his own bed wench for the evening. He narrowed it down between Babbs from Belize and Susie from Suriname. It was a win/win either way he went.

"Sup. You asked for me? Fifty bucks a song, a 'hunnit for private show," Diamond announced when she arrived. Pop was stuck on the plump mound of pussy in her boy shorts, so Jax spoke up for them both.

"How much to take you to a room and run a train on you? A grand? Two-grand?" Jax said, killing all the excuses she had on her mind. Snake just forced his dick in her mouth for free earlier, so fuck his rule about leaving with customers. Besides, the party girl only lived for the moment and two grand would buy a couple moments.

"Three grand since its two of you," Diamond said trying her luck. If they declined she'd settle for the two.

"Bet," Jax said and stood. Pop was still stuck wondering if she had a hamster or gerbil in her boy shorts.

"Let me go change," she said shooting a guilty glance around. The place was packed and the night was young so she could go fuck these two to sleep and make it back before closing.

"Black Lexus truck," Jax informed her and led his partner back out the club.

"He leaving," XL announced just in case his boss had went blind. Snake just looked at him and shook his head.

"He'll be back," he said and sipped his drink knowing Jax would return before he reached the bottom of it.

****

"There she go!" Pop said meaning here she comes when he saw Diamond sneak out the club. She looked around and Jax flashed his lights to get her attention. She nodded and made her way over to the black truck and got in.

"Sup," she greeted and closed the door behind her. She slinked down a little since she was out of pocket by leaving early.

"You," Jax replied and passed a smoldering blunt to the back. Pop was too excited for words and just stared at her legs.

"Here you go player," she said spreading her legs so he could see what he was after. To his delight she'd ditched the boy shorts in favor of her usual commando preference. She rarely wore panties, opting to give her vagina a chance to breathe since it took a lot of abuse and therefore needed the fresh air. Pop blinked in awe of her bare box as they pulled off.

Jax bent a few corners and ended up down by High Bridge at the Old Motor Lodge that had seen better days. She frowned at his choice knowing the place was run down. She would know too since she'd turned a trick or two there before. Pop didn't give a flaming fuck, long as he got to fuck the exotic woman.

"Get a room. I'll be up in a second," Jax said, pushing a crisp hundred towards him. He pushed a stack of cash towards Diamond to quell any complaints she may have had. She gave it a quick count and hopped out behind Pop.

Jax retrieved his sandwich bag of coke once he was alone and took a few bumps. A few minutes later Pop texted the room number and he hopped out. Jax knew there were no cameras in the parking lot but still kept his head down so no one could see his face. He made his way around back and up to the second floor. Once he found the room he paused to listen through the door. He only heard Pop since Diamond had her mouth full. He tried the lock and the door opened.

"Yo! She got some..." Pop proclaimed until Jax fired a shot at his tonsils. It blew the rest of the compliment out the back of his head. Diamond turned just in time to see the flash that sent her wherever Pop had just gone. At least Jax let her keep the money and quickly fled the murder scene.

****

"He's back," XL reported when Jax entered the club for the second time. This time it was news since Snake was busy interviewing the newest dancer. The 19-year-old shook her tight, young ass in front of the man hoping to earn a spot on the coveted center stage. Only the baddest of bad bitches got the top honors. They were the ones who got to work the VIP section with all the ballers. It meant the difference between leaving with a few hundred for the night or a few thousand.

"Mmhm," he agreed without taking his eyes off the tight little caramel clam between her legs. He reached forward and touched it and it soaked his fingers. A taste of the sweet juice got her that much closer to her goal.

"Sup yo?" Jax inquired and frowned at the new girl. He hadn't seen the pretty young thing before and instantly put her high on his list.

"Just...chillin," Snake replied lazily and ate a little more honey from his fingers. "How was that?"

"A-fucking one! That shit cooks like a dream," he admitted. It was too much information but he was excited. He should have proclaimed it 'a'ight' and said 'I've had better' but so much of it coursed through his system like truth serum. "Oh! I got a gift, for you."

"Nice," Snake said admiring the brand-new plastic polymer pistol in a box.

"Only fired twice! "Jax bragged leaving off that it was fired into the back of a cop's head. Pop certainty couldn't say anything since he was leaking brain matter on a motel floor.

"Cool. Thanks. Grab you a broad and have some fun," he said and stood. The bulge in his pants indicated he planned to do the same. He pulled the young girl by the hand. She giggled at not having time to put her bikini back on as he dragged her away like a caveman.

Snake took the teen into his office and locked the door behind them. He sat her on the leather sofa and unzipped his pants to free his raging erection.

"Dang!" the southern belle rang seeing his manhood throb. She got a brief reprieve from the pounding it promised when he dipped between her firm legs. "Ssss."

"Mmhm," he agreed as he sucked on her young pussy. He realized then he didn't stand a chance inside the girl. If he had that much trouble getting his tongue in her it would be a struggle to get his meat in her. Accordingly, he reached down and stroked himself as he ate her.

The girl came twice before a nut spewed out the tip of his dick. She frowned, slightly grossed out from the warm semen hitting her body. She took a deep breath and braced herself as he took position between her legs. Luckily for them both the nut took a little steam out of his erection. He wrestled himself inside and quickly reached another orgasm.

"What's your name, little girl?" he asked when he caught his breath again.

"Laffy Taffy," she giggled. Even she knew her late grandmother didn't have stripping in mind when she gave her the nickname as a toddler.

"No, your name. Your real name," he insisted.

"Daphine," said of her rarely used government name. Only people from her Phenix City, Alabama hometown knew it. She'd fucked and sucked her way up north to become an actress.

"Well, welcome to Back Shots! You gone be a headliner!" he advised. They celebrated by her giving him some head.

Chapter 14

Life without my father was immediately different. My mom was always distant when he was away from home but now that he was never coming back we both went our separate ways in the same house. Me, I dived deeper into the safe world of books and research. I had no idea what my mother was into but whatever it was, wasn't good.

"I'm rich! I'm rich!" Michelle sang and danced with the insurance policies in her hand. It was in poor taste but in her defense, she was quite drunk.

Rohan had a hundred-thousand-dollar policy from New York City and an additional hundred grand personal policy. His mortgage insurance would pay the house off as soon as the claim went through. His family was set for life. Should have been, could have been. Good thing for his mother he had a separate policy for fifty-thousand in her name as well because Michelle wasn't giving her a penny.

"Uh oh!" she whined when she realized she was at the end of the eight ball she copped the night before. Only right since she had been chipping away at it since the night before.

The six-hundred of the eight-hundred-dollars she still had brought a smile to her face. Anytime she had some extra cash from some extra source she would trick it off. She'd gotten into trouble for using household money for her own frivolous shit. It suddenly occurred to her that she never had to worry about that again. That being said the decision was made to drive into the city for more drugs.

"I'm not doing anything?" Megan said fearfully when her mother popped in her doorway.

"Well, don't cuz I have to run out. Don't answer the phone or door cuz it won't be me," she advised.

"OK, Mommy," the girl replied, noticing the woman had on the tight little shorts she had gotten in trouble for wearing. It was here first indication that everything was about to change. "Can I have something to eat?"

"Cook... Here, order a pizza or something," Michelle said fishing out a fifty. She didn't notice the frown on her daughter's face at the contradiction. How was she supposed to get a pizza if she couldn't open the door?

Megan shrugged and took the money. She switched from one of her nerdy websites to the local pizza shop. The chubby girl felt like a kid in a candy shop looking at all the toppings and side dishes. Fifty bucks was plenty so she ordered to her heart's delight. Her dad used to make her watch what she ate but he wasn't here anymore.

****

Michelle wanted to bypass Reese altogether so she wouldn't have to share her coke but she didn't know little Wop's phone number. She knew the dealers in the courtyard would have served her but that was too public. Her mom would hear about it before she got to inhale one line. The last thing Dianne needed was an excuse to start using again. Besides she didn't plan on seeing her mom so she came the back way to Reese's apartment.

"Shit!" Reese fussed at the knock on her door. She had all the company she was expecting and he was delivering picture perfect back shots.

"One...second, ma. Just...hold...up!" he pleaded feeling a tingle in his toes. It spread up like an electric current, increasing in intensity with each stroke. His eyes rolled and his head lolled when he reached the point of no return. His body seized as he climaxed inside of the well-used vagina. "Argh! Mmm! Shit! Whew!"

"Who?" Reese yelled while he was still pumping her full of his seeds. "You straight?"

"Me!" Michelle yelled back as she listened through the steel door. She let out a little chuckle at the sounds of sex. She cared less about interrupting because she was trying to get high.

"I'm good," her vaginal guest sighed and pulled his wet dick out of her. He looked around for something to dry it off with as she jumped up to pull her shorts and shirt back on. Finding nothing else he used a doily from the table and put it back. He barely had his meat away when she snatched the door open to let her guest in.

"Girl, what happened to you?" Reese fussed as if it was she who left her.

"Bitch, please! I seen you leave... Sup, Black," Michelle greeted seeing her old friend. His presence explained the scent of sex floating in the air along with the weed that served as foreplay.

"Sup," he replied. "Catch you guys later."

"OK, bye!" they both sang and waved until he departed the apartment.

"Girl, you still fucking Black?" Michelle asked in mock astonishment. She'd fucked him once or twice herself but that was more than twenty years ago when they were all teens.

"Hell yeah! Dick still thick and he still keep that loud. Anyway, what you doing back out this way?" she answered and asked since it was rare for the woman to be seen so much in the hood.

"Had to see my moms. Just wanted to stop and, yeah, you seen Little Wop?" she asked once the bushes were thoroughly beaten around.

"He prolly in the courtyard. You ain't see him when you came through?" she asked headed to the sofa to peer down to the court yard. Michelle noticed a wet spot on her shorts as gravity pulled the semen back out of her loose vagina. "He out there. Yo, Wop! Come up!"

"I ain't even see him," she said and sat on the chair, assuming that the wet spot on the sofa correlated to the one in her shorts. "I may as well cop a little blow while I'm here."

"I know that's right!" her friend cheered at the concept of free get high. It would set the free weed off just right. They lied to each other for the few minutes it took for the dealer to make his way up stairs.

"Yo, I gotta get cash, I..." Little Wop explained he wasn't tricking tonight until he saw Michelle in the room. "Sup, ma?"

"You. I need a couple of them eight balls. Oh, and a gram too," she said. Reese cut her eyes at her knowing the gram was coming her way while she left with the rest. She should have been grateful for the free coke but she lacked gratitude. Section 8, food stamps and Medicaid had spoiled her into thinking she was supposed to get everything for free. The government crutch had handicapped her.

"Here you, go..." Little Wop said and he produced the dope from different pockets. He counted the cash along with Reese and tucked it away. "I'm out. Holla back if you need anything else."

"OK," the two friends sang as he left. Michelle sprang into action since she didn't plan on staying herself.

"Here, I gotta bounce!" she said urgently and pressed the extra gram in her friend's hand.

"Yo, where you going? Chill. Hang out," Reese said as her friend rushed from her apartment as well. She was still trying to stall her when the door closed in her face. "Bitch!"

"Yo...Wop. Hole up!" Michelle called as she caught the young dealer in the stairwell before he got outside.

"Sup, ma?" he asked with a curious frown. Surely, she wasn't going to suck him off for coke in the exact same spot her friend did. In an ironic twist Reese sucked his daddy off for coke in this exact same spot a couple decades back.

"Yo, I ain't tryna have err body in my business. Give me a number or something so we can link up. I'ma need like an ounce or something next time," she said while he pulled out a pen and paper.

"I got onions for a grand, nine hundred for you tho. Get at me, ma," he said handing over his digits. A good ounce customer is better than a blow job if you're a real hustler.

****

"The fuck?" Michelle groaned when her alarm clock started talking shit from her night stand. Technically, it just buzzed according to the time she'd set, but it sounded abusive after just one hour of sleep. She slammed her hand down on the snooze button as if it was the clock's fault she stayed up snorting coke all night.

Michelle made a mental note to buy some weed today too. Something to balance the coke so she wouldn't be up watching infomercials all night. The clocked buzzed again as the ten minutes sped by. She let out a deep sigh and hoisted herself up. A few blinks later she remembered exactly why she was up and rushed into the bathroom. She peed loudly and hopped into the shower. Once she was dried and dressed she emerged from her lair.

"Good morning, Mommy," Megan greeted hopefully. Hoping for some affection in her time of grief. Hoping for some breakfast like most days.

"Did you eat?" Michelle asked, indicating she didn't plan on cooking. She cooked for her husband and her child got to eat. He was gone now so the child was on her own.

Sa'id Salaam

"No, I thought you..." she began but didn't make it to the end of her statement.

"Thought I what?" she huffed with an indignant chuckle. "Thought I worked for your fat ass? Well I don't! I keep that bitch full so you can at least feed your damn self!"

Michelle was still cursing as she stormed out and got into her truck. She was plenty high already but still took a few bumps since it was a good ride into their city. She turned the radio up and danced in her seat as she headed downtown to sign insurance papers.

"Well..." Megan said trying to reason why she should or shouldn't eat ice cream and cake for breakfast. She would have loved the bacon, eggs and etcetera, her mom cooked for her and her father but didn't know how to make them. Cold cereal was so cold, so ice cream and cake it was she decided, nodding her head.

After, 'breakfast' she headed back to her room to get ready for school. Dressing was the easy part since the school required uniforms. She pulled a fresh set of the required yellow shirt and green dress from the cleaner's plastic wrap and got dressed. Her mom usually did her long hair but she was already gone. Megan didn't care enough about appearance yet to try to do something with it and set out for the bus stop.

"Not you catching the bus?" a girl said faking shock. Most of the kids' middle-class parents had to work to keep their middle-class status so their kids caught the bus.

Megan strained her eyes at the girl trying to figure out why she was talking to her. The only friends she had were online so she only communicated with teachers at school.

"She think she all that," another girl explained. They spent the ride to school getting ignored as they talked about her. Megan immersed herself in her school work to mute the fact her father was dead.

****

"And here?" Michelle asked cautiously as she carefully signed the insurance paperwork. She still found it hard to believe she was about to be given a couple hundred thousand dollars. Even she knew she couldn't be trusted to do the right thing with all that money. She felt slightly guilty at what she knew was coming.

"OK. The mortgage check will be sent directly to the bank," an adjuster explained. She checked to make sure she signed in the right place before handing two checks across the desk.

"OK," Michelle agreed. She felt some sort of way about the house being listed in her daughter's name instead of hers. The ten-year-old was now a homeowner but she had racks on racks. She only glanced at the checks before putting them in her purse. All she saw was zeroes and that was good enough for her. She needed to get up out of there before they figured out she wasn't shit.

Michelle ignored the nag of her high coming down and forewent taking another hit. She didn't even turn the music on as she headed back out to Long Island. Her breathing returned to normal when she pulled into the bank parking lot.

"OK, girl, just be easy," she coached herself as she entered the bank and got in the line. A few minutes later she reached the counter and smiled.

"Good afternoon, Mrs. Robinson," the teller greeted and smiled back. "I'm so sorry to hear about your husband! He was..."

"I need to cash these checks," she cut in on the condolences. She just knew she was doing something wrong and wanted to get up out of there.

"Cash?" the woman asked in astonishment when she saw all the zeroes. Who walks around with two hundred thousand dollars in cash.

"No?" Michelle asked reading the woman's face. She could tell she didn't think it was a good idea.

"You probably don't want to have so much cash on you? Why don't we deposit them minus some cash?" she suggested softly.

"OK. Umm, gimme ten thousand and deposit the rest," Michelle decided.

"Yes, ma'am," she agreed and completed the transaction. She had plenty of coke so she headed to their mall to shop.

Chapter 15

The day of my dad's funeral was the worse day of my life. As bad as it was my life was about to get worse. As sad as it was my mother's behavior was just too much. I swear I hate funeral; especially cop funerals.

Megan hated wearing dresses in general but found herself staring down at yet another dress for yet another funeral. She wasn't a tomboy but she wasn't a girly girl either. All she required was comfortable clothes to nerd out on the computer or in a book. Her extravagant mother bought her a new black dress, shoes, hat and hosiery to see her father off to the hereafter. Michelle had shopped every day since her husband's passing, returning from the mall with bags upon bags of new clothes and shoes. Mostly shit for her to party and hangout in but they both got new funeral outfits.

"Hmp," Megan said at the frilly new training bra. She was more overweight than top heavy and hated bringing attention to herself. She looked at herself in the mirror and shook her head the spectacle in spectacles. The hose had a fishnet pattern and black patent leather shoes with a three-inch heel. The dress dipped in the front for cleavage she didn't have and didn't quite make it to her knees. It was way too much for a ten-year-old.

Shaking her head privately would be her only protest since she didn't want to risk another beat down. Her volatile mother stayed coiled like a cobra ready to strike at any moment. She went into the kitchen to fend for herself and eat breakfast. Being left to her own devices packed more pounds on her already chubby frame. She followed direction on the back of a box and made a pretty red velvet cake last night for dinner. She only ate half so the other half became breakfast.

"Mm, mm, mm," she moaned and did a happy food dance as she devoured the cake. At least the milk she chased it with was somewhat healthy. Was, until she added copious amounts of strawberry syrup and a scoop of ice cream to it. Breakfast alone would pack two more pounds on her round frame.

Megan knew her dad's death was a big deal since it was all over the news. She'd noticed the extra police presence but never equated it to any potential danger.

The high-profile case meant his funeral would be a big deal as well so she couldn't figure out why they weren't headed towards the city yet. The smart girl knew exactly how long it took to reach Manhattan from Suffolk county. The next click of the clock meant they would be late. Not a good look since they were a part of the circus that is a cop's funeral in the city.

Megan wanted to wake her mother up but that would mean her mean mother would be awake. The woman had become more verbally abusive by the second so she kept her distance. The phone began to ring pretty regularly courtesy of someone insistent upon being heard so she hoped it would wake her up.

"The fuck! The whole, damn fuck!" Michelle cursed at the ringing phone. Whoever it was obviously wouldn't take the hint that she was ignoring them. She rolled over and snatched it off the receiver and barked. "What? What could be so damn important you blowing my shit up?"

"Hello, Mrs. um, Robinson. This is the Captain. Um, the funeral starts shortly and I um... We..." he stammered wondering why the fuck she wasn't there yet.

"Oh yeah. Well, go on without me. My um, car won't start, so yeah..." she said ready to hang up. The captain's next words coincided with the chiming of the doorbell.

"Yes, I um...figured it was something like that so we sent a car for you. She should be at your door now?" he said knowing she was since she'd notified him when she arrived. Plus, the doorbell could be heard chiming in the background.

"...OK," she groaned accepting defeat and hung up. Michelle realized she'd passed out fully dressed when she rolled out of bed. She looked good in the designer duds she wore to meet Lil Wop and cop more coke. She let out a howl of relief when she sat down to pee. "Whew!"

"Mommy, the door!" Megan called from the bedroom door. She had been cursed out lately for so much she was scared to answer it.

"So, get the damn door!" she shot back and flushed. "Stupid ass bitch act like..."

Megan shook her head and twisted her lips as she went to answer. She had been cursed up and down for answering the door for a neighbor just yesterday. A sense of relief swept over her when she saw the uniformed police lady standing at the door. Her first thought was that the woman was there to save her.

"Hello, I'm Officer Davis. I knew your dad. He was... Are you OK?" the cop questioned seeing the distressed look on her face. The trained peace officer saw she was in need of being rescued.

"Yes," Megan heard herself say externally as she screamed for help internally. Stockholm syndrome stifled her plea for help. "My mom is in the shower."

"OK, dear. You're so pretty in your dress," the woman sang even though she wondered why it was so short. It was like a little girl's club dress.

"Thanks," she replied feeling awkward. Her mother came out of her room several minutes later in a matching dress, hose and high heels.

"Let's go cuz I can't be out here all day," she fussed instead of greeting the woman or thanking her for the ride since she was still high and legally drunk. The couple hours of sleep she'd gotten were no match for the amount of drugs and alcohol she'd consumed. It would take a mini coma for her to regroup from her solo party session. The officer fought not to frown and lost. Michelle didn't miss the condescending grimace and said so. "He dead, yo. Standing around all day ain't gonna bring him back."

"I'm so sorry," the cop told Megan once more. The first one was for the loss of her dad, this one for having a fucked-up mother. Both she and Megan shared the secret wish that they were going to her funeral instead of his.

Once they got going Michelle put her large, black designer glasses on and took a nap leaning against her daughter in the back seat. Meanwhile, the cop used her lights to bypass all traffic and traffic laws to get to the funeral. Megan stared off in shock trying to see her cloudy future. It seemed so bright just days ago, but now she couldn't see past the car window.

"Excuse me ma'am, we're here!" the officer called out when they arrived at the church. It took several more calls and honks of the horn before she awoke.

"Shit!" Michelle fussed at being woke up once again. She wiped a line of drool away and climbed out. She smiled seductively when she saw the outstretched elbow ready to lead her inside. "Thank you."

"My pleasure," Jax said extending the other to Megan. Megan reeled as if it were a snake and cowered behind the lady cop.

"Come on, I'll walk you in," she offered since she felt the same way about the flashy young cop. She felt some kind of way about the flirtatious look him and Michelle shared on the way into the church for her husband's funeral. They were seated next to Rohan's mother and Angel but neither acknowledged the other. Megan and Angel shared an understanding frown at both losing a parent. The only parent they'd had since Angel's dad was down south and Megan's mom was busy flirting.

****

Michelle fell asleep again behind her shades once again as the preacher preached. A large picture of a smiling Rohan stood next to his casket. It was to remind loved ones of happier times because he didn't look happy at all laying in the box.

Jax stole glances down Mitchell's dress and admired her plump breast. He gazed down at her firm thighs and shook his head. He just knew his old partner hadn't been hitting this right. A side glance got a dirty look from her daughter and set his eyes straight again.

Megan broke protocol and went to stand by the casket. She wanted to be close to him and away from her. She stared down at her father looking restless in his eternal sleep. A procession of police began to file by paying their respects even though some weren't very respectful.

"Poor bastard," a red-faced cop muttered and crossed himself. He shook his head a final time and walked off. Men and women cops, beat cops and brass all lined up to see him off. Jax took up the rear since he was his partner.

"Look at you, still sleeping," he said sarcastically. "Tried to put you on. Tried to make you rich, but no, you wanna be super cop. Well, look where that got you. Stretched out in a box."

Megan overheard the disrespect and added it to her distrust and hatred of the man. Little did she know her father felt the same way about him. Little did she know he was the reason he was flat on his back in the box.

"'Bout damn time," Michelle muttered when it finally came time to head out to the grave site. She wasn't looking forward to the bag pipes or the twenty-one-gun salute, but the sooner they put him in the ground the sooner she could go get high. Her mind flashed to the cocaine laced blunt she'd left in the ashtray and made her smile internally. A glass of wine, a blunt and a vibrator where her plans for the day.

The mild withdrawals of her fledgling addiction nagged at her like wondering if you turned the stove off. You're pretty sure you did but just what if you didn't? She had some coke in her purse despite half the New York City police force being present. Narcotics agents had been hugging her and giving her condolences despite her being dirty. The opportunity to take a hit never arose she had to sit there sober and take it.

The tears looked genuine when the cameras panned on the grieving widow and child. The reality that her dad was never coming home hit home hard causing Megan to sob deeply while snot ran from her nose. Michelle was just bored to tears and ready to go. She just wanted to make it home before videos came on so she could sing, dance and get high. The thought of now being able to hit the clubs again bought an inappropriate smile to her face.

She fell asleep again on the ride out to the cemetery. He and Maria had grown up together so it was only right they were buried side by side. Megan didn't know it yet but the blank space next to his grave was reserved for her. His mother and wife had plots as well but they were on another row. Side by side as well to his amusement.

Finally, Michelle thought to herself when the show came to an end. At least she thought it was a thought until she saw the look on her daughter's face and realized she'd spoken aloud. She shrugged her shoulders like so since one, she'd meant it and two, the girl couldn't beat her.

"Yo, can I get a ride home? That broad drive too slow," Michelle explained to Jax in front of Officer Davis.

"Sure," he agreed and led the way to his car. The lady cop hated to see the little girl leave. The look on her face when she opened the door would stay on her mind. She decided to make it a point to check on the girl in the near future.

Jax pushed the music to the rear speakers so the child couldn't hear the grownup conversation in the front seat. It was verbal foreplay as they bantered playfully the whole way out to Long Island. She was refreshed from all the sleep she got during the service and ready to turn up.

"So..."Michelle said inviting him inside of her when he pulled into the driveway.

"I got some business to handle, but if you need anything just give me a call later," he said accepting the offer and passing her his card. Michelle almost leaned over to kiss his lips until her forgotten child moved behind them. They shared a glance that set the date to fuck first chance they got.

"I'll call you later," she assured him and got out his car. She put a little extra in her walk as she walked to the door to make sure he took that call.

Chapter 16

"Yo, that nigga Pop got found dead up in the Bronx!" one of Jax men announced when he entered the spot. His eagerness to share news didn't go unnoticed by Jax or Mano.

"Say word? What happened?" Jax asked while Mano stifled a laugh. He knew the second they got the news that Jax popped him. It now made sense why he had the weak link put in the work. Then had him leave his work behind at the spot. It would get divided up and distributed amongst the survivors.

"I heard he was with some married bitch?" one speculated. He hadn't heard shit but wanted to be heard. He didn't realize the character trait made him the next crash test dummy in line. There's safety in silence and people should learn to shut the fuck up sometimes.

Jax nodded contently as they speculated, knowing this would be what the streets were saying. He was happy to hear all the wild speculation that steered any suspicion away from him. He was ecstatic that each had moved an entire kilo of coke in two days. There were plenty of deals and specials but it was gone and that's all that mattered. He planned to flood the streets of Brooklyn until it overflowed into Queens, Manhattan, Staten Island and finally the Bronx. Once he made it up into Snake's borough he would no longer be needed. He would get his connect and murder him and his help.

"You niggas, did your thing last night I see!" Jax cheered with the stacks of racks on the table. He pulled more coke out the bag making them just as it happy as he was. The money was placed in the empty bag once a nod from Mano confirmed their counts.

"Sup for tonight?" Mano inquired as they all donned their mask to cook coke.

"May head out to the Island or hit the club. You riding?" he asked moving back away from the stove.

"With you? Hell no!" he cracked knowing how Pop ended up after a night out with the boss. The rest of the men laughed even though they didn't get the inside joke. When the boss laughed, they laughed. It's not technically dick riding since he cut the checks.

"Guess, I'll head out to the Island then," he shrugged like fucking his dead partner's wife after having him killed and killing his killer was no big deal. It wasn't the worst thing he'd done in life nor was it the worst he would do. He was still young and had plenty of fuck shit to pull. All in a day's work for a monster.

****

"See, that's why your big ass is as big as you are!" Michelle snapped when she found Megan making yet another cake for dinner. Megan had counted on her mother staying cooped up in her room doing whatever she does and took a chance on making a cake. She didn't count on the aroma reaching her room and awakening her munchies.

"But I..." Megan began but a vicious back hand knocked the excuse out of her mouth. She ducked the follow up blow having learned they came in twos. Luckily her mother woke up hungry enough to cook. Unluckily it came with a beat down and verbal abuse.

"Bring your fat ass around her so I can teach you how to cook!" she demanded. Megan moved tentatively just in case she got swung on again.

The smart girl practically memorized every step as her mother prepared macaroni and cheese for the oven then fried chicken in a Dutch oven. Green beans came from a can and rolls out of a container that made Megan jump when it popped.

"Scary little ass! Girl, you wouldna made it growing up in my projects! Niggas shooting err day. Bitches fighting, cutting with razor blades. Shit, I remember when Reese gave this bitch a buck fifty over her own man!" she fondly reminisced. The cognac she sipped made her happier and drunker by the sip.

It was a twisted bonding session as the mother taught the daughter how to cook with a busted lip. By the time the food was prepared both were smiling and laughing like days gone by. Megan had been taught that alcohol was bad but realized it made her mother act good. A lesson was learned that there can be good in bad. The duality of creation, everything in pairs. One day she would learn how to apply the lesson to her own benefit.

"You're so pretty!" Megan heard herself admit as her mother's smile lit up the kitchen.

"I? Thank you, baby! You are too! Just wait 'til you lose this baby fat. All the boys gonna wanna hit that!" Michelle cheered.

"Thank you," she said mainly because she didn't catch the inappropriate part of the compliment. They fixed their plates and sat down at the rarely used dining room table. Fried chicken and macaroni and cheese trumps most conversations so they ate in silent nods and smiles.

"I shoulda made cake for desert!" Michelle announced once the plates were empty. This was her first real meal after a two-day coke binge.

"I can, if you want me to?" Megan asked despite just getting slapped for trying to make one.

"OK, baby. I'll be in my room," she agreed and rushed off in her tiny shorts. The sleep and food had her soberer than she cared to be so she hit her supply. "What, shall, it be?" Megan wondered as she perused the selection of box cakes in the pantry. It stayed stocked with everything a family needed to eat and drink. For now, anyway because Michelle became less domesticated by the day. A double chocolate cake winked and whispered to get her attention. "Oh, you want us to eat you? OK!"

****

Megan smiled at her handy work once she'd literally put the icing on the cake. It looked as pretty as the picture on the box and she was quite proud of herself. She cut two large wedges out of it and placed them on saucers. Two matching glasses of milk was poured and desert was served.

"It's ready, Mommy! The cake, is ready!" she called down the hall towards her mother's door.

"Too late now," Michelle giggled since the coke had snatched her appetite away. She took another hit on a joint laced with powdered cocaine and held the smoke deep in her soul.

"Mom..." the girl called until the chiming of the doorbell cut her off. She frowned at the time on the clock and doorbell, knowing they didn't go together. Her father shut the house down at ten PM so who would come calling at eleven?

"Who is it?" Michelle asked looking just as confused as her daughter. She used to sneak out her mother's apartment with boys back in her day but knew her nerdy daughter wasn't about that life.

"I don't know?" she shrugged and followed her to the door. Michelle's butt cheeks protruded from the bottom of the tiny gym shorts and wiggled as she walked.

"Who?" Michelle called out then smiled at the man through the peep hole. "Go to your room."

"My...room?" she asked more confused by the goings on than word room.

"Your room, bitch. The pink frilly palace you live in," she snapped causing her to take off. Michelle watched her

149

disappear around the corner then opened the door. "What brings you here?"

"Told you I'd stop in and..." Jax began but her nipples poking through the thin T-shirt along with the camel toe in her shorts made him lose his train of thought.

"Mmhm," she laughed snatching his gaze up from her snatch. "Follow me."

Jax felt his dick jump when she turned and walked away. She walked heavier than normal to put some bounce in her exposed ass cheeks. Jax made up his mind to bite the left one as they went. Megan peeked from her cracked bedroom door as she led the man into her room. She was too naive to be angry but wanted her cake and milk. She was prepared to sneak into the kitchen as soon as the door closed. Michelle swung the door closed behind her but it remained slightly cracked. Megan was undeterred and hit the floor. She slithered along like a chubby snake towards the kitchen. She ignored the muted conversation as she slid past her parents' room.

"What brings you way out to the suburbs?" Michelle asked again once they were seated on her bed. Jax looked around and took in the decor as well as the cocaine laced weed aroma lingering in the air before he spoke or rather used body language as he leaned back and unzipped his pants.

"What am I supposed to do with this?" she quipped, grabbing his dick for inspection. She gave it a few strokes causing it to throb to life. She squeezed and tugged on it until she held a full-fledged erection. She mentally compared it to her husband's and then Greg's. The thought that she had her husband's partners dick in her hand didn't stop her from leaning in and taking it into her hot mouth.

"Figured you knew what to do with...mm, it," Jax moaned. He kicked his two hundred dollars sneakers off to begin the undressing.

"Mmmm," Michelle moaned when he reached down and played in her soaked pussy. Her mouth was too full of dick for words but he got the point. She tugged his jeans off with him still in her mouth like an acrobat while he lifted his shirt over his wavy head.

"OK," he said when she came on his hand. As good as her hood pussy felt on his fingers he couldn't wait to get his meat in her.

"You gotta eat it first," she warned as he rolled a condom on his erection.

"Picture that," he laughed and positioned himself between her slippery lips. "I beat, not eat."

"Ssss. Well, beat then!" she urged as he began to sink inside of her. She and her dead husband's partner locked eyes when he rested his dick head against her cervix.

Jax gave a curtsy and commenced to digging her out. There was no tenderness, kissing or caressing. Just bed bouncing, skin slapping, grown folks fucking. Just the kind of hood loving she never got in this bed. It wasn't long until she howled in delight from the first of many orgasms to come.

"Yes!" Megan called out thinking she heard her name. She felt a little guilty when she polished off her cake and milk then started on her mother's. She listened but never heard her again so kept on eating. She kept right on eating until half the cake was gone. She was full and sleepy when she finally finished gorging on double chocolate and milk. She forgot her mom had company as she staggered back towards her room. Until she neared her cracked bedroom door that is.

"Flip over," Jax demanded and took his dick out of her life. She quickly complied so she could get it back in her life. She assumed the position and arched her back. Her vagina puckered up and allowed hin easy entry into her insides.

Megan blinked, rubbed her eyes and blinked again as she peered into her mother's room. She of course knew what sex was in theory, but this was fucking and it blew her mind. The combination of sights and sounds froze her in place. She didn't necessarily want to see it, but couldn't pull herself away.

"Mm-mm," Michelle declined, shaking her head no when he rimmed her anus with his thumb. Her mind shot to back in the day when Ray-Ray came home from a bid and introduced the projects to anal sex. He was sexing all the girls before he went to prison and came home with a fetish he'd picked up in the big house. Her, Reese and the other hood rats didn't get the ramifications of a dude returning from jail looking for anal sex. They got the picture when he fucked a couple of guys too. Michelle may have declined verbally but made no attempt to stop him from inserting the digit in her rectum. When his thumb entered she came instantly.

"Where you think you going?" Jax teased when the orgasm collapsed her flat on her belly. He followed and kept right on stroking. Megan cocked her head curiously when he began slamming in and out out of her. "Shit, mm, I'm coming!"

Megan wondered what that meant but only for a second until they demonstrated what it was. He pulled out and pulled the condom off while her mother flipped back over onto her back. She reached out and stroked his dick until it exploded on her stomach and chest.

"Mmm, all that," Michelle admired as he skeeted all over her. Jax opened his mouth to reply but saw Megan's shocked face. His shock registered on his face where Michelle found it. "What?"

"Nothing," he replied as the girl backed away. He neither knew how much the child had seen nor did he give a fuck how much she'd seen. He was here to fuck and fuck he did. "Ready for round two?"

"Let me take a break to powder my nose," she said and retrieved her coke from her nightstand. Jax watched her inhale coke up each nostril and knew he'd be hanging out here more often. A lot, more often.

Chapter 17

"What?" Michelle finally asked when she caught her daughter staring at her again.

"Nothing," Megan replied and quickly snapped her head away. She was looking for some change in the woman after watching her have sex the night before. She still looked the exact same even after the night of sex. She didn't watch anymore after Jax caught her, but she'd continued to listen to the sounds of sex until the wee hours of the morning.

Jax had joined Michelle having a few lines between bouts of sex. He knew not to use too much and render himself a limp noodle. They alternated weed, coke and sex until dawn when he finally left.

Michelle looked pretty much the same, except she had a little extra pep in her step and song in her voice. Almost the same as after her late husband had laid some really good pipe. Jax had a little more pipe and laid it a lot better resulting in the woman up cooking brunch and humming love songs.

"Pay attention, trying to teach you how to cook. As much as you like to eat..." the mother teased.

Megan took the teasing in stride just like she did in school. Being constantly bullied gave her pretty thick skin covering her low self-esteem. Besides, she knew she needed to learn how to cook more than just boxed cake. Even she'd noticed she'd packed on a few more pounds.

Bad Cop

Michelle bantered brainlessly and aimlessly as they peeled potatoes and chopped onions for home fries. By the end of the session, the girl knew how to fry home fries, scramble eggs and make the crispy, crunchy bacon she loved. A definite win followed by another win when they got to eat it.

"Well, I'm going shopping. Clean this kitchen," Michelle announced and stood. Megan wanted to ask to go with her but decided not to push her luck. Besides her mother always purchased her miniature versions of the hoe clothes she now favored. She couldn't dress like a slut when her husband was alive but he wasn't now. Instead Megan cleared the table and tackled the mess they left behind.

Meanwhile, Michelle lit a joint to join the lines she made on the night stand. Her stash was depleting, signaling a trip into the city was in her near future. She looked at Jax's phone number and wondered if or when she should use it. A twinge of regret said no then a throb of her vagina said yes. Next thing she knew her phone was in hand and she leaving a message on his voicemail.

****

Jax awoke on the sofa with his daughter's mother standing over him, cursing him out in rapid fire Spanish. He didn't need to speak the language to know what the hot-blooded Latina was mad about. He'd stumbled in a few hours ago smelling like sex with a hickie on his neck. She'd really be mad if she saw the trail of passion marks leading down to his worn-out dick.

Usually he could appease her with his penis but he had nothing left after the night inside the widow. He did the next best thing and reached for his jeans on the floor beside him. Too tired to count, he passed her the whole wad of cash inside. Maritsa frowned at the roll of cash curiously. Even she knew it was too much. She usually got a couple grand to turn off her Telemundo theatrics but this was closer to ten.

"Hmp!" he urged so she would take it and go. He needed some sleep after making his rounds early that morning. He would have to make them again in a few hours then again that night. Having that much work on the street required being hands on. He trusted Mano but the workers still needed to see his face.

Maritsa snatched the cash and their daughter and tore out of the apartment. Jax did a half roll on the sofa and went back to sleep. He awoke several hours later and lay still for a moment to put the previous night in perspective. A smile spread on his pretty face when he recalled the episode with Michelle.

"Poor fellow left all that good loving behind," he said sarcastically of his late partner. "Don't worry buddy, I'll keep it hot and gushy. I promise to make her come every chance I get."

****

"Sup yo?" Jax inquired when he walked into the stash house even though he already knew. He had five more kilos in his bag because he knew his team had sold out. Word was spreading throughout the borough about the good coke at great prices. Other dealers tried to cut prices to compete but their product couldn't fuck with Jax's.

"Getting rich out this bitch!" a worker cheered. They were moving so much coke it made up for the discounted price. That meant more money in their pockets.

"Shit booming," Mano reported. "Got niggas from Queens coming through. Give me the word?"

"Word!" Jax greedily agreed. He was ready to step his game up which meant a trip out to Back Shots. Good thing he stayed fly so he wouldn't have to go change.

Jax supervised the cooking of coke and paid a bonus to D-rock for best whip game. Mano actually won again but Jax was smart enough to spread it around. Everyone was eating and happy which kept everyone loyal.

"I gotta bounce out to the Bronx," Jax announced when it was time to take his leave. He gave a few pounds before lifting pounds of cash onto his shoulder. His phone began to buzz as soon as he got into his car. It almost went ignored until he saw the new number with a Long Island area code. "Mrs. Robinson, I presume?"

"How you know?" Michelle wondered with a tipsy giggle. Jax felt his dick jump just from hearing her voice.

"Sup wit' you, ma?" he asked instead of answering. Again, he already knew the answer but still wanted to hear her say it.

"Come see me?" she said pouting through the phone line.

"Why?" he kept on with the rhetorical questions. He knew she wanted some more meat just as bad as he wanted to give her some.

"So, you can make me come," she shot back since she never was shy; especially when it came to dope and dick. She hoped he'd deliver both so she wouldn't have to drive into the city.

"As much as I would love that, I can't tonight. Got business," he explained as he navigated the Bronx streets towards Back Shots. "Rain check?"

"Rain check," she agreed reaching for her shoes. As soon as they hung up she called Lil Wop to tell him she was on the way.

****

XL spotted Jax as he walked into the club. He puffed his big chest out in pride since Snake had left him in charge. The new girl had him so open that he spent more nights at home stretching her tight vagina out. Like many men a cute young girl would be his downfall.

"Peace," Jax greeted giving XL a pound when he reached the VIP section. He glanced around for the boss as they shook hands but didn't see him. "Where's Snake?"

"At the crib eating some Taffy," he replied quite amused with himself. "I got your work in the office. Where the bread?"

"In my car. I'm parked out back," he explained since he didn't want to walk through the club with hundreds of thousands of dollars. The veteran girls would smell all that cash through the bag and attack.

"Bet," XL agreed and led the way to his boss' office. He used the key and let them both inside. The coke sat on the desk in a neat pile of bricks bringing a smile to Jax's face.

"This calls for celebration! Order us a bottle!" Jax ordered knowing the man was used to taking orders.

"OK!" he agreed and took off just like he knew he would. Jax wasted no time once XL left him alone in the office. He checked the drawers and rifled through the papers. He pocketed anything with an address then checked the walls for a safe.

"Jackpot!" he cheered when he found it behind a MTA subway map in a frame. He smiled at the cheap dial knowing a couple strokes with a hammer would open it up as easy as a line of coke opens a stripper's legs.

"Dom P!" XL proclaimed when he returned with a bottle of bubbly. He popped the cork letting it hit the ceiling like they just won a championship.

Once the bottle was empty they completed the transaction of trading dope for dollars. Jax put his hit list on hold for later and left the club alone. He drove at a leisurely pace since he had enough coke in his trunk to put him under the jail. Once it was secured in his house he headed back out to his car to go over the papers he stole from the office.

"Bet my life this is it!" he announced when the same address appeared on a couple of the papers. He checked a map and charted a course back out to the Bronx.

****

"Let me see," Snake said moving Daphine's weave out of his camera shot. The newly installed braces glistened as she gave him a blow job in slow motion. The teen had consumed most of his time and semen since she pranced into the club. She was so young and green he decided to keep her for himself.

"Mmm," she hummed as he went stiff and pumped her mouth full. It tasted like yet another shopping spree so she gladly swallowed it down.

"Shit! Fuck! Sss!" he cussed and fussed while Jax mounted a tracking unit under the bumper of both of his cars.

"See you soon, Snake," he nodded and smiled as he pulled away. Now all he had to do was wait until he led him to his connect.

Chapter 18

Officer Davis couldn't shake the look of distress on Megan's face when she met her at the funeral a week ago. Sure, it was her dad's funeral but the blank look in her eyes told a deeper story. She wanted to report her to child protective services but they required more than just a strange look in the eyes. That's why she decided to drive out to The Island personally to check on the girl.

Megan had just finished eating tacos she'd made herself. The upside to her mother staying high was that she was always happy. She happily taught her daughter to cook and even braid her own hair during these sessions. She turned into a monster whenever she got sober but luckily, she had enough money to stay high.

A snarl spread on Megan's face when the doorbell began to chime. She just knew it was that nasty man who came and did nasty things to her mother at night. It wasn't night yet so she took a chance and checked the door.

"Hello! Remember me? I drove you and your mom..." Officer Davis sang, leaving off the part about the funeral.

"My mom is sleep," Megan replied. She didn't have the same look of desperation in her eyes but it was replaced with sorrow which is just as bad.

"Can we get something to eat?" she asked knowing the big girl must like to eat. "Is there a good place to eat around here? I'm starving!"

"The buffet?" she asked hopefully since she hadn't been since her dad died. She knew the consequences of going out without permission but this was the buffet so she was willing to risk it. Besides it was just noon and her mother wasn't due until at least three when videos came on.

"Sure, OK," she agreed even though it was clear the girl was doing something she shouldn't be doing. She was experienced in interviewing children and would pry everything she needed to hear from before she finished her first plate.

Megan slipped out and softly closed the door behind her confirming the cop's suspicions. The cop asked about the neighborhood as drove through just to get the girl talking. It worked too as Megan told everything she knew about everything and everyone as she gave turn by turn directions to the all you can eat.

"Umm..." Officer Davis wondered when Megan began to pile her plate high with meat and potatoes. She held her tongue assuming she probably wasn't eating well at home. She was actually eating plenty, she was just greedy.

"The chicken is the best," the big, little girl said with a chicken and a half on her plate. She joined it with some pot roast, macaroni and potatoes.

"No vegetables?" the health-conscious cop asked as she designed a colorful salad on her own plate.

"Oh yeah," Megan agreed since she strove to be agreeable at all times. Once they were seated with their drinks Davis steered the conversation inside the house.

"So, how are you and your mom making out since your dad is not here anymore?" she asked, dancing around the D word so she didn't lose her. The word dead can dead a conversation in an instant.

"Fine, I guess..." she began between a combination bite of chicken and beef. "I mainly do the same thing I always did. Read, study and stuff."

"How are the potatoes? What does your mom do? Probably sad, huh? Crying and stuff?" she pressed.

"Fine, no. She and her boyfriend stay in her room doing... stuff," she said, frowning up to show what she thought of whatever this stuff was.

"Do you like her new boyfriend?" Davis asked fighting not to react about the woman having a man around her child so soon after the death of her father. Michelle had been immediately cleared as a suspect but this revelation was suspect as hell.

"Jax is OK, I guess. Are you OK?" Megan reeled when the lady cop choked on her cola.

"Jax as in Detective Jackson? Your dad's partner?" she croaked, trying to recover from fluid going down her windpipe.

"Jax," Megan shrugged since she didn't know anything about the detective part and kept on eating. The cop was too disgusted to finish her meal but the resilient child quickly cleared her plates. "Can I have desert?"

"Sure," the cop agreed as the wheels turned in her head. This was something or could be nothing. Either way she planned to get to the bottom of it.

"Will you come back?" Megan practically pleaded when they arrived back at her house. She didn't budge awaiting on the answer.

"I sure will, soon," she assured her. She watched the girl wobbled up the steps and ease inside as stealthily as she'd left. "Very soon."

Megan was relieved to smell her mother hadn't awakened when she returned. The lack of weed or menthol smoke in the air said she was still sleeping because she as soon as her eyes opened.

****

"Don't put your finger in my ass again," Michelle purred and wiggled her ass so Jax would do just that. He did and got the same results and it pushed her over the edge. "I'm coming!"

"I'm, right, ugh, behind, you!" Jax grunted literally and figuratively as he pounded out some solid back shots. This time there was no condom to remove so he let go inside of her. She told him it was his pussy so he treated it like it.

"I'm coming?" Megan repeated wondering what it meant. She heard her parents have sex on occasion in the past but they never shouted about I'm coming. "I'm coming," she repeated it once more as she typed it into the search engine.

Her eyes went wide and fluttered when the results popped on the screen. She didn't tell her finger to click the mouse and start the video but that's what happened. Megan cocked her head curiously as a white lady had a head thrashing orgasm at the end of some guy's tongue while screaming I'm coming!

"Eww!" she fussed without turning away or clicking off. She couldn't figure out from the woman's contorted face if she was in pleasure or pain. It got even more confusing when the man slid up and slid his erection inside the woman. She looked down the hall realizing this is what was going on in her mother's bedroom. What she didn't know is what was going on outside.

"Yup, that's his car," Officer Adams, Davis's partner, agreed as they eased down the street. Partners fuck each other's wives all the time so he wasn't quite as convinced of a murder plot as she was.

"Need we guess what he's doing her?" she quipped.

"I'd say, back shots," he nodded with his bottom lip poked out. He recalled the widow had a nice ass so that's the approach he would have taken. "It's not a crime though?"

"Should be," she said and hopped out. Her partner shook his head as she crept forward and dipped under Jax's rear bumper. He held his breath hoping she didn't set off the alarm as she attached the tracking device. She popped up a second later and rushed back to the car.

"It won't stand up in court, you know," Adams reminded when she returned.

"It won't have to. We just need to see where he goes and with who," she replied then turned to peer at him. "Not unless you tell him. Is there something going on that I need to know about?"

"What? No! I just don't think one has anything to do with the other. The woman was twerking at the Christmas party. Her boning a handsome young guy ain't a stretch to me," he shot back in indignation as he should have. Anything less and she would have suspected him as well.

"Yeah well..." she said at a loss for words since she recalled the spectacle. She remembered feeling bad for Rohan who'd looked utterly embarrassed when his wild wife turned the party out. The ride back out to the city was made in silence as both cops wrestled with their own thoughts.

****

"I gotta take this," Jax said seeing Mano pop up on his phone. Michelle playfully clamped down to keep him in her mouth. She almost had him hard again for round four. He pried himself free and answered the call. "Sup yo?"

"I followed dude and think I know who his plug is," Mano said enthusiastically. Jax looked around for a place to talk in private but found none. He had no doubt she would press her ear to the door had he stepped into the adjoining master bath.

"I'm gonna step out on the deck," he told her and opened the door. Michelle knew the man shouldn't be walking around her house naked with her daughter home but didn't try to stop him. Instead she leaned over and took another hit.

"Uh oh," Megan said hearing footsteps coming in her direction. She knew she would be in trouble for being online in the den instead of tucked away in her bed. Trouble once met a scolding and no cake, however, now it came with lefts, rights, kicks and curses.

She dipped behind the sofa and got out of sight. She expected her mother was on a mission to quench her drug fueled thirst but heard a man's voice. Curiosity got the best of her causing her to take a peak. The bobbing penis captured her attention and held it like a hypnotist pendulum. She ran her eyes up and down his slender, muscular frame as he stepped out on the back deck. Her eyes locked in on the large tattoo covering most of his back. A very detailed globe surrounded by the words The World is Mine.

"OK, now tell me what's up," Jax demanded once he thought he was clear from prying ears. Little did he know he was being both watched and heard.

"Yo, I followed that tracking device and watched him go to see the Dominicans up in Westchester. Son, this definitely the plug!" Mano said excitedly. Not quite as excited as Jax who felt his dick jump from the good news.

"That's what's up! Looks like ole Snake's services are no longer needed," he proclaimed grabbing his manhood in his hand. He gave it a few slow strokes as he spoke. "I'll be in the city in the am. Bout to go fuck the Mrs. silly. I would have killed my partner sooner if I knew his wife pussy was this good!"

Megan was frozen in her place from both the dick in his hand and the words that just came out of his mouth. She'd barely got out of sight when Jax turned and came back in. He frowned at the rustling from the sofa but stopped short of investigating. Instead he pulled on his erection and rushed down the hall.

Michelle was busy snorting more coke when he rushed back in. Her nostrils were in use but he still slid back into her mouth. She finished powdering her nose and gave him full attention.

"Come on and ride it," he decided and laid on his back. He picked the smoldering blunt from the ashtray to smoke while he watched the show. And what a show it was when she turned her back to him and slowly sank on his dick. She found a comfortable place and began to rock and ride. Ride, roll and rock until a puddle formed under her.

Megan was relieved not to get caught and eased back to her room and closed her door. She could hear the sexual symphony of moans, whimpers, and bed squeaks through the closed door but Jax words reverberated in her mind. The man in her house, in her mother, killed her father.

Chapter 19

Jax believed Mano about the plug but drove up the Westchester county just to see for himself. The gated estate had multi-millionaire written all over it. A couple million in automobiles embellished the circular drive as proof. Several discretely armed men nonchalantly guarding the premises spelled that this was indeed the plug. Jax ran a few license plates.

"Armando Ruiz," he practically cheered as the vehicle registrations came back to a notorious yet untouchable drug lord. The state of New York had pretty much given up on building a case against the man. No one would testify and he never kept any drugs anywhere near him.

Snake had visited him on occasion to talk business, yet business was never conducted here. That meant more surveillance to find out where the deals were consummated. XL alluded to making moves for the boss before he could re-up soon.

Jax drove back down to the Bronx and swung past Snake's house. His cars hadn't moved since he hadn't been anywhere other than Daphine's insides. He was so sprung on the young girl he was letting the help handle his business. Jax wasn't the only one doing surveillance, however.

****

"So, just how does a detective afford such trappings?" Davis asked sarcastically as they checked out a brownstone owned by Jax. It was worth a couple million, so even the mortgage should be out of a cop's range. Not to mention the new cars parked out front.

"Um..." Adams replied since he didn't have an answer for the questions. What he did know was the Porsche truck was sick and he secretly wanted in on whatever Jax had going on. He let out a love-sick sigh realizing whatever it was, was doomed since his bloodhound partner was on the job.

"Exactly!" she shot back since there was only one explanation for his riches. "Jax is a bad cop!"

"So, you think, he had something to do with Robinson getting wacked?" he asked incredulously.

Bad cops literally come a dime a dozen in the city. Everyone got something for free some way somehow. He'd received hundreds of free blow jobs when he worked vice. She ate free meals at a Chinese takeout in exchange for running the dope boys away. Perks, tips, or whatever, everyone was doing something, but killing a partner was crossing the blue line.

"I don't believe in coincidence. I..." she paused to check her ringing phone. She frowned at the number but took the call. "Hello?"

"He killed my dad. He said it, I heard him," Megan whispered even though her mother wouldn't be up for hours. She was still in a drug and dick induced coma that wouldn't break until videos came on.

"Who, baby?" Davis asked and squinted as if it would help her hear better. "Oh wow. How'd you hear this?"

"He was here last night," she recalled, feeling embarrassed at looking at his penis. She could still see it when she closed her eyes, along with his sleek muscled frame and large tattoo on his back.

"Listen. Don't say anything, to anyone. When he comes over you stay in your room. You hear me!" she barked louder than intended, then softened. "OK, baby?"

"Yes, ma'am. Are you going to put him in jail?" Megan asked hopefully, hoping her mom would go too.

"I am. You don't say anything to anyone," she reiterated.

"What?" Adams needed to know. The woman's yellow face was white in shock.

"That was Rohan's daughter. She heard Jax admit to killing her dad. Time to talk to homicide."

****

"Time for a homicide," Jax said to himself as he pulled up at Back Shots. He realized the best way to get next to Snake was to eliminate his help.

"Hey Jax!" the hostess sang as Jax breezed in. Word had spread about his plumbing skills and she was eager to have him come to her home and lay some pipe.

"Sup, ma?" he asked her breast then looked to her mouth for the reply.

"You. When we gonna hang out?" she pressed, putting her hands on her hips to demonstrate the spread.

"Soon," he replied, meaning as soon as I kill your boss and take this joint over. He didn't catch her reply since he was already heading towards the VIP section, smiling spread across his face at seeing XL in Snake's spot doing his best Snake impersonation. He sipped Cognac while two dancers danced on each side of him like thots in stereo.

"Jax," he cheered just like Snake would and raised his glass.

"Sup yo. That looks good on you. You a boss for real," he said, gently stroking his ego.

"For real?" he asked so eagerly both girls frowned and twisted their faces.

"Can you, ladies, excuse us?" Jax asked with crisp hundreds since they worked better than twenties. They snatched the money and ran leaving the men alone. "Bruh, I see what's going on and I want in," he leaned in and whispered.

"You do?" he asked with a curious frown that almost made Jax crack up. The fact that he didn't know meant he was open to being told. The man was a human remote-control ready to change life's channels on demand

"Hell yeah! You the next boss and I'm your side kick. Shit, you do all the work anyway," Jax said and paused to let the slow man digest that before moving on. The man's slow head nod suggested he was digesting it just fine so he moved on.

"You do all the work but he gets all the glory and all the money. What he paying you, ten grand a week?"

"Five!" XL shot back feeling slighted. Like twenty thousand a month for standing around was chump change. It was only now that Snake stayed laid up with the young girl that XL made buys and ran the distribution.

"Shit, take over and I'll work for you for six a week? When is the next buy?" he pressed since he had him wide open.

"I gotta meet with the Dominicans tomorrow. Why don't you ride with me?" XL offered, as if had been his own idea and not the fruit from the seed planted by Jax.

"Hell yeah! I'll be your side kick," Jax added and sealed the deal since everyone wants a sidekick.

****

"What's wrong with you? Why you ain't in bed?" Michelle asked when she found Megan standing behind the sofa in the exact same place she saw and heard the naked man laugh about killing her father.

"Nothing!" she shot back since the rage didn't quite compute in her young mind. Neither did replaying her gaze up and down the naked man's body.

"Well, take your ass to bed," she fussed since the man was on his way over to get naked. Michelle shook her head as she watched her chubby daughter waddle off down the hall. She grabbed a bottle of liquor and a couple of glasses.

She retreated to her room to prepare for her date. Not much preparation since they were just going to fuck. She showered and selected a sexy nighty from her daily shopping sprees. The fool had parted with over fifty thousand dollars on clothes and drugs in the weeks since her husband's death.

"Here's our boy," homicide detective Marinetti announced as Jax rode by. He proved his suspicions were correct when he pulled into the grieving widows drive way.

"He's got that walk!" his partner Pascal noticed as Jax walked to the door. Men take on a distinct swagger when some pussy is imminent. It was confirmed when Michelle opened the door wearing a see through something.

"Damn!" Jax proclaimed his approval and scooped her into the air.

"Damn!" Marinetti seconded when see wrapped her thick legs around his waist.

They began kissing and groping as he carried her through the house. She reached down and freed his erection before they made it to her room. They were still in the hallway when she wriggled it inside of her.

"Shit!" Jax fussed when the good, hot pussy engulfed him. He couldn't take another step and leaned against the wall. He picked her up and dropped her on his dick repeatedly while she wiggled and rocked. The commotion brought Megan to her door to investigate. She opened it and got an eye full.

The sex was so urgent neither registered the little girl feet away and continued fucking right there on the spot. Their sex was always mutually satisfying but it was Michelle who exploded first tonight.

"I'm, come...come...coming!" she explained. Jax threw it into over drive to help get her off. Megan now knew what that meant but still couldn't tell if it was pleasure or pain.

"Uh oh", Megan thought to herself when Jax shouted he was coming next. She knew what that meant too and scrunched her face up at the memory of the video she seen. She knew too that's where babies were made but was lost when her mother hopped off and drank those babies. It was all too much for her so she eased her door closed again and went to bed.

"Did you bring me anything?" she asked as she escorted him into her bedroom. She still had plenty of her own drugs left but liked free drugs better.

"But of course!" he replied and produced a bag of coke. "I'm chilling tonight, I got a thing in the morning."

Michelle gave a more for me shrug and dumped some on the night stand. Jax took the liberty of completely undressing and climbing into his deceased partner's bed.

Chapter 20

"Did we ever check this?" Marinetti asked holding up Rohan's cell phone in the evidence bag. He found it in the box of evidence, but didn't recall reading a report on it.

"Nah, battery was dead when we got it," Pascal explained with a shrug.

It made his partner wonder for the hundredth time how he ever became a detective. The man had to be urged and nudged in every direction like a cow. Marinetti just shook his head and plugged the phone to a charger. No one ever wants to believe a cop killed another cop but that's how it was starting to look. One thing for certain was Jax was crooked. The tracking device tracked him to several known drug spots with known drug dealers but not a single arrest was made. Nor was there any record of any active investigation. If nothing else, it proved he was on personal not professional business.

"Good idea! Why didn't I think of that?" the dimwit nodded. His partner pressed his lips together tightly so the offensive reply wouldn't escape.

"Well, let's take it in. I'm sure our boy is sleeping in today," he suggested since they'd spent the night staking out the Robinson house. Jax bounced around inside the woman all night but was up and out first thing in the am.

What they didn't know was that Jax was fueled by 100% pure Columbian cocaine. He took a power nap still inside of Michelle for a couple of hours and got back on the go.

****

"That's two million. Wanna count it? Nah, it'll take you a year to count that high," Snake teased as he passed XL a satchel full of cash.

Laffy Taffy giggled like the goofy teen she was. Her plans to dance her way to the big screen were put on hold for a moment by her newest sugar daddy. It was a steady supply of sugar daddies who'd gotten her this far towards her goals. She figured why spend years in college and working when she could come up a lot faster by tricking and twerking.

Snake was spending real good and digging her out even better so she'd decided to ride it out as long as possible. Most of that riding came in the form of reverse cowgirl with Snake filming it on his phone. The dick and dough were right so she hovered around like a slow, moving cyclone scooping up whatever wasn't nailed down.

Not unless he fucked around and left that safe he'd shown off open and left the house. All she needed was a few minutes to clean him out and move on to California. Snake liked to show off the million he had saved from dealing but it also held millions more owed to his connect. That would be his problem if he ever fucked around and left it open long enough. He slept too lightly to get him in his sleep although she tried on several occasions.

"I don't need to count it. I can count though'," he said stoically. Snake heard the different tone but was too arrogant to make anything out of it.

"A'ight then, my nigga. Handle that and put everything in the stash house. Take care of Jax and dude from the Island..." he instructed. Tasks he knew how to handle all too well from handling them for months.

XL nodded and shot a glance at Daphine as he collected the money. She popped her legs open and closed really quick to give him a parting shot of her plump, bald vagina just in case number two ever moved up to number one. Unlike Snake she recognized the look in the man's eye. A look she was all too familiar with from seeing it in the mirror every day. The look of unbridled ambition, the most dangerous emotion in creation.

"Round three?" Snake invited and washed a Viagra down with his whiskey and cola.

"Four you mean." the girl giggled on her way down to help the pill work. She kept one eye open and watched the open safe as she worked her head, lips and tongue. Soon she held a whole erection in her mouth and round four commenced.

****

"That's two million. Wanna count it?" XL bragged when he met Jax at the club. He left out the insult as he did his best Snake imitation.

"Nah," Jax said, turning his lips down in disdain. The money was worthless compared to meeting with the connect.

Besides, he knew it wasn't his money so showing it off was futile.

"OK, don't say nothing to no one," XL coached as they walked towards his car. It was the same speech Snake gave him way back when, when he first put him on. "You like, my security."

"So, I better drive then. Can't have the boss driving the help, can we?" Jax suggested like a Jedi mind trick. He steered him over to his car to put his plan in motion.

"Yeah, oh yeah!" he agreed nodding his big head and followed Jax to his car. XL frowned at the painter's tarp covering the leather seats. "Sup with the plastic?"

"Huh?" Jax replied since the man wouldn't appreciate the truth. He changed the radio and subject letting the big man speak. And speak he did. XL bragged aimlessly as they rode while Jax recorded it all mentally and on a digital recorder.

"We meet Flaco and Junior twice a month. A hundred bricks each time. The money is dropped off first, then we make the pick-up..." He laid out Snake's entire operation as they rode. Jax poked his bottom lip out and nodded to the good and snarled at the bad. He would adopt some and reject the rest.

"I see," Jax agreed following his turn by turn directions until they reached China town. They stopped in front of an old-world China restaurant with dried ducks hanging in the front window. The kind of Chinese restaurant that doesn't serve wings and fries in greasy bags like in every hood. "What's here?"

Sa'id Salaam

"Flaco. This is where we drop the dough," he explained then hopped out. Jax followed him inside the restaurant and towards a back table.

"Who this?" Flaco frowned at the breach of protocol. He didn't flinch because several of his shooters did.

"New help," XL explained, sounding just like his boss with truncated answers.

"Jax," Jax greeted and extended his hand. The man examined it for a second then took it.

"Flaco. I'll see you around," he said accepting his presence, knowing he'd been cleared to make it this far. XL passed off the satchel of cash and turned to leave. It would be counted and confirmed by the time they reached their next stop.

"Where to next?" Jax asked when they were back in his vehicle.

"Brooklyn!" XL barked like a boss would do. Jax smiled when he heard his home borough announced. Moving on his turf made his plan that much easier.

"Say word! What part?" he asked as they pulled from the curb. He glanced in the rearview to see if they were being followed. His smiled widened when he saw that they were. XL picked up his banter as they rode off to the next borough.

****

183

"Here we go. In there," XL directed as the gate of an auto garage opened in response to his text message.

Jax nodded as he pulled past an armed guard on both sides. His trained cop eyes shot in all directions, taking it all in. What he didn't see XL narrated as he gave up the whole operation.

"That's Junior," he said sounding in awe of the well-dressed young man. One glance showed he was the boss's son. The flashy young man wore a ton of jewels and the smile on his face indicated whoever was on the other end of his call was pleasure, not business. New pussy Jax presumed by the look in his eye.

"I'll hit you back, mama?" Junior frowned curiously at the new face. He let out a slight chuckle at the chick's retort of hitting her from the back instead of hitting her back. "Yo, who dis?"

"Jax. He works for me now," XL explained. He was getting used to being the boss already as he made the introduction. "Junior, Jax. Jax, Junior."

"Sup yo! Bout time ole Snake got some new blood!" Junior cheered. He shot a quick snarl XL's way showing what he thought of the man.

"Word!" Jax shot back. He saw the same ambition in the man's eyes as he had seen in his own. He was almost where he needed to be. Junior was the missing link.

The two young men bonded as they made small talk about cars, guns and which club had the hottest women while 220 pounds of cocaine was loaded into the trunk. XL smiled and nodded, trying to be a part of the conversation but was too old to catch most of it.

"You coming next time?" Junior asked once his workers closed the trunk.

"Two weeks," Jax agreed nodding since they had bonded just that quick. "Matter fact...take my number."

XL was thirty-eight hot when the two men exchanged numbers and agreed to hang out later. He now second guessed his decision to let the man tag along. He and Junior never kicked it, or made plans to hang out.

"Let's go," XL barked louder than needed to let everyone know he was the boss. Jax and Junior shared a *yeah right* chuckle and dapped each other up. They got back in the car as the gate rolled back up to let them out.

Jax looked around cautiously as he pulled out onto the street. He saw the same car that had followed them there pull out behind them. Knowing the streets of Brooklyn so well allowed him to deviate from XL's directions.

"I said left!" he barked, still in boss mode when Jax bust a right instead.

"Short cut," he shot back, watching the tail turn behind them. "We got company."

"Shit!" XL fussed and turned completely in his seat. He caught on when the car took the same left and following right. Jax suddenly pulled over and came to a stop. "What are you doing?"

"Robbing you," Jax explained from behind a pointed pistol as Mano hopped out of the car behind them and ran up.

"Snake's going to kill you!" he defiantly declared. "You're a dead man!"

"You first," Jax laughed when Mano pulled the door open. XL opened his mouth to protest but Jax fired a round into it.

"This a big nigga!" Mano grunted as he pulled the large corpse out of the car by the plastic tarp. He dumped him in the gutter below and hopped in the passenger seat. "We out!"

****

Snake twisted his lips as he checked his phone once more. The deal had been done hours ago so he couldn't understand why XL hadn't checked in yet. His customer from Long Island called complaining about his package several times but he had no explanation.

"What's wrong, Daddy?" Daphine asked with a sexy pout when she saw he wasn't watching her show.

"Nothing. Keep dancing!" he ordered and called the man's phone again. Again, it went to voicemail, but his line beeped before he could leave yet another scathing message. "What!"

"I got your dope, is what," Jax dared and waited. He wanted to feel him out to see what his next move would be. "Your boy gave me the whole shipment on a side deal."

"Meet me at the club!" he said and stood. Snake rushed into his room to dress for the first time in days. Laffy Taffy frowned curiously as he stormed out of the house. She rushed to the window and watched him pull out of the driveway. As soon as he bent the corner she rushed into the bedroom.

"Shit!" she fussed when she saw he'd locked the safe. She shook her head and snapped her fingers like, "I'ma catch you slipping ole man."

****

"Do you hear this!" Marinetti exclaimed and ran the recording back. Pascal was so engrossed with the naked pictures of Michelle he'd missed it.

"The fuck?" the slow cop said when he heard Rohan's last words before two slugs shut him up forever.

"Jax was there! Call the captain!"

Chapter 21

"This is no coincidence! No fucking way!" Marinetti barked at the Brooklyn murder scene. "The tracking device puts Jax right here at the time this guy gets popped!"

"Then, the recording?" Davis reminded. Jax's voice was clearly heard on the tape right when Rohan got shot. Proof that he was present at the scene despite the statement's he gave about being home.

"Hmp?" the Captain pondered. He furrowed his brow, looked at the detective, down at XL and back to Marinetti. "Pick him up!"

"What about her? She has something to do with this!" Davis insisted of Rohan's not so grieving widow. She took it upon herself to surveil Michelle on her many shopping sprees and drug runs. The woman was having the time of her life instead of mourning the loss of Rohan's life.

"Pick her up too," he decided despite not having a warrant. Hopefully, she would incriminate herself so he could get one. Davis didn't need to be told twice and took off like she had been shot out of a cannon. She used her police lights to speed out to Long Island.

Meanwhile, Michelle was high as a satellite, dancing to the radio in her room. She had just returned from yet another shopping spree to buy more clothes. She couldn't figure out why the designer duds she'd just bought a month ago didn't fit anymore. Most likely because she'd consumed more cocaine than food. The only protein she got came in spurts from the end of Jax's dick.

Megan managed to maintain her weight since she could now cook whole meals. She did the only cooking in the house and Michelle ate once a day before she started getting high for the night.

****

Snake was still calling XL's phone when Jax walked into the club. He hung up immediately and pointed at him. On cue club security rushed to his side to escort him to the boss.

"Easy fellas, I'd hate for you guys to go meet XL," he warned. The men were unfazed since they didn't know the large man was laid out in the gutter ready to be zipped inside a body bag. Snake stood and stormed towards his office knowing the men would follow.

"Where's my shit!" Snake howled in a high-pitched voice. Fear combined with anger caused a little of the bitch in him to slip out. Even he heard it and cleared his throat to try again. He had a right to be scared knowing how Ruiz did business. "My shit, nigga, where is it?"

"Safe. Your boy XL cut me a sweet deal. Too sweet so I knew it was some fuck shit and called you," he explained quite reasonably as he wiggled away from the goons. "If, I was on the bullshit why call?"

"I want my shit!" Snake insisted. The last time he'd visited Ruiz the man showed him a videotaped beheading of a middleman, just like him, who'd lost a shipment, just like him. He had no way to explain being pussy whipped by a tight young pussy while his man handled business. There was no excuse for it and he knew it. "Where is it?"

"I'll deliver it where..." Jax started, holding back a smirk. Snake exploded once more just like he knew he would.

"No!" he screeched letting a little more bitch slip out. Jax shot a glance to his men to see if they heard it. Twisted lips and shaking heads said they did and didn't like it. "Take us to it!"

"OK," Jax shrugged and headed for the door. "You guys wanna follow me or..."

"No! You're riding with us," Snake insisted as they exited the back door. He and one of his goons got in front while the other got in back holding Jax at gun point. They pulled out of the lot just as the first police cars followed the tracking device to arrest Jax.

Jax made smart comments and small talk as they navigated through the Bronx and Manhattan. He gave turn by turn directions instead of the address of the final destination. The suspense amused him immensely; especially Snake's frustrations.

"Brooklyn? Why are we going to Brooklyn?" he whined when they crossed over the Brooklyn bridge. "We coulda took the Throgs neck and been there by now."

"Oh yeah," Jax chuckled and gave more directions. Snake's brow furrowed when he recognized the neighborhood.

"Next right. There's a white garage door halfway down the block on your left."

"That's... that's Ruiz's spot! How you...? Why..." Snake asked as the door began to roll up. He turned to face Jax for explanation but only got a smile and smirk. Luckily Junior was there to explain.

"Snake!" the son's boss greeted with a smile when his man opened the door on the truck. Snake stepped out looking confused when his own men put their guns away and stood next to Jax.

"Oh, they with me. Better pay," Jax said in response to the questions etched in the man's face.

"And, he's with me," Junior explained, explaining the rest. "We had a long talk and decided you old cats are in the way. You, my dad, and the rest of you old niggas are just old fashion. That's why me and my mans here gonna do things a little different."

"Yup. No more middle men. We the plug, distributor and street sales," Jax confirmed. "In other words, your services are no longer needed."

"Wait! Hold up! I'll pay you!" Snake pleaded as Juniors men led him away.

"I need a body," Jax leaned and explained to Junior. He repeated it in Spanish to his men causing their heads to nod. Junior needed the body as well to explain to his father why the man had been replaced. They would use the missing coke to finance their new joint venture. Blaming Snake for the theft gave a reason to murder him.

"Look forward to doing business with you," Junior said extending his hand.

"Likewise," Jax replied as they shook. He and the guards got back into the truck and pulled off.

"Let me go home! I'm calling your father!" Snake yelled as he was being loaded in a van to be driven off to slaughter.

"Wait! Hold on!" Junior ordered when he heard mention of his father. The same father who'd abused him and his mother most of his life. The same father he planned to overthrow in a coup de gras. "You wanna go home?"

"Yes! Keep the dope, keep the business. I just wanna go home," he pleaded. He had plenty of bread and some nice, tight meat from down south. They could have it and he'd retire.

"Take him home..." Junior directed spreading a smile on his face. Snake let out a sigh of relief but it wasn't long lived. "Then kill him."

****

Megan frowned at the ringing of the doorbell. It was too early for Jax to come over, but he was the only one who came calling. She kept right on eating prepared to ignore it.

"Your fat ass don't hear that bell?" Michelle fussed as she traipsed out in a designer mini skirt. She did a verbal drive by, spitting insults on her way to the door. Assuming it was Jax making a daytime dick delivery she tossed in, "Cock blocking ass."

"Mrs. Robinson?" Officer Davis asked officially, even though she knew who she was. She wished she could add *I have a warrant for your arrest* but couldn't since she didn't have one.

"We need you to come downtown to answer some questions."

"Now?" she squealed incredulously and looked at the clock. "I'll come out tomorrow. I gotta go see Lil Wo...I mean, my moms anyway.

"Ma'am, we need to speak with you now. Unless...you have something to hide about your husband's death?" she dared, cocking her head.

"Fine!" Michelle huffed and turned to Megan. "Get dressed. We're going to the city."

"OK, Mommy," she agreed and put on her sneakers. She followed the women out to the unmarked police car and got in the back seat with her mother.

"Can I smoke?" Michelle demanded on her way to lighting a menthol.

"No," Davis managed without losing her cool. She was a smoker herself but wouldn't smoke in front of a kid; especially someone else's. Michelle huffed and puffed as she made a big deal of putting the cigarette back into her designer purse. Moments later she was snoring lightly for the rest of the ride. She didn't wake back up until they arrived into underground parking lot.

"Can I go to my dad's desk?" Megan asked once they reached the precinct. She always loved looking around

Rohan's desk at the wanted posters as well as pictures of herself.

"Not right now," Davis replied since the desk had already been reassigned. Instead, she was taken into a room set aside for children. The place they waited for grandparents or social workers to come collect them after some tragedy. She was a little too old for the selection of toys but managed to busy herself with a coloring book. Once she was settled the cop turned back to Michelle. "You, come with me."

"I know you need to watch how you talk to me," Michelle fussed as she sashayed behind her. Her swaying hips drew lots of eyes as guys remembered how she put on at the Christmas party. Her and Jax's inappropriate affair was the talk of the precinct, but no one could blame him since they wanted her as well.

"In here," the cop ordered as she opened the door to an interrogation room. She would have loved to cuff her to the table like any other perpetrator but she wasn't under arrest. Not just yet anyway.

"I ain't got all day," she shouted as the woman left her alone. As bad as she would have loved to question her this was a homicide case so she went to get the homicide detectives. Usually a perp is made to stew in his or her own juices while waiting to be questioned but she was here on her own and could leave whenever she felt like it. For that reason, they didn't keep her waiting.

"The grieving widow is in room 3," Davis said to Marinetti at his desk. "Mind if I observe?"

"Not at all," he replied and stood. His useless partner stood as well and followed him to room 3 while Davis went to watch from behind the two-way mirror.

"Smug bitch!" she growled as she watched Michelle primp her hair and pose in the mirror. She was here to talk about her husband's death yet she was busy checking her booty in the glass.

"Mrs. Robinson," Marinetti announced as he stormed in the room. "I'm detective Marinetti. This is my partner detective Pascal."

"Hey," she greeted flirtatiously to Pascal since he was licking her up and down with his eyes.

"Hey," he blushed and giggled to his partner's embarrassment.

"Have a seat," he demanded to them both as he took one himself. Pascal sat beside him as she sat across from them. She did a slow-motion leg cross that showed she wasn't wearing panties and kept a neatly shaved box. Pascal giggled once more but his partner stayed focused.

"Did you have Jax kill your husband?"

"What?" Michelle asked and frowned. "What's that supposed to mean?"

"What else could it mean?" he answered with a question as he pulled her husband's phone. The curious look on her face showed she recognized it off the bat. The detective paused her by holding up a finger and played a snippet of the recording then asked, "Who was that?"

"My husband. Now, what that got to do..." she replied until he cut in with the same finger and another snippet from the recording.

"And who is this? I'm sure you know the voice since you're sleeping with him," he dared and peered at her.

"That's Jax but we ain't sleeping together. We're fucking, but what's that got to do with you? Or my husband getting killed," she snapped hotly.

"Now, let's hear it all together," he cut in again and let it play. The room went silent save the conversation between the two partners. These were Rohan Robinson's final words. It culminated in the gunshots that put him on the elevator to the upper room.

"Oh, my God!" Michelle broke quite convincingly. The cops looked at each other to see if the other believed the break down. Michelle was some bullshit in general but both believed the tears were sincere.

It was now crystal clear to her as well that Jax was involved with her husband's death. A hell of a thing to find out after she found out that morning that she was pregnant by Jax.

Chapter 22

My life changed once again and once again for the worse. As bad as it was, things went downhill pretty quickly. Sugar to shit is was its called, and now I understand why. Sadly, I knew it would get worse, just had no idea how bad it would get.

"Mrs. Robinson?" Marinetti asked after letting her bawl for several minutes. It was now clear to him and even Davis watching from the next room that she wasn't involved in the murder. She was a smut bucket, a thot perhaps, but she wasn't a killer.

"Man," Davis groaned when the interrogation came up empty. She hated to have to let her go, hated to have to drive her all the way back out to Long Island even more. She let out a deep sigh and went to have a word with Megan.

"Is my mom in trouble?" Megan asked when the cop walked in on her coloring session. Her tone was more curious than concerned as she pondered who would take care of her. The choice between grandmothers twisted her lips curiously. Oddly her paternal grandmother seemed to be the better choice. Mainly because she could play with her cousin but also because her maternal grandmother had beaten her out of her whole allowance. She really felt some kind of way about it after she researched the different games when she got home. The old lady made up a few rules as she went along and got down on her.

"Not yet," Davis heard herself say before correcting herself. "No, but the man who hurt your dad is."

"Jax. Is he under arrest?" she asked hoping he wouldn't be coming back to her house anymore. "He didn't hurt him, he killed him. I heard him say so!"

"Not yet, but he will be soon. We're looking for him now," she assured.

****

"So... I mean, you sure? But why?" Michelle moaned. She had just passed or failed a pregnancy test that morning so the news devastated her. In her drug polluted mind, she and Jax were going to be together since she was carrying his child. She snared Rohan with her pussy trap and thought she had another one.

"You heard the recording. He may not have pulled the trigger, but he's just as guilty," Marinetti explained. His partner kept a vigil on her thighs hoping they would part again so he could see her vagina once more. It sure looked a lot better than the old beat up one he had at home.

"You ready? I'll take you home," Davis announced as she stuck her head in the door. Pascal's eyes blinked rapidly as she uncrossed her legs and gave him what he'd been waiting on.

"You can just drop me in the Bronx. At my mom's," Michelle sighed. She was way too upset and sober to have to go all the way out to the Island to get high. She was low on drugs anyway and needed to see Lil Wop.

"OK," she eagerly agreed. The woman stood and followed her out and down to where her daughter was waiting. Then to everyone's surprise she reached down and hugged her daughter.

Davis snarled angrily when Megan initially flinched from the sudden movement. It was a clear sign of someone who has been abused. The little girl had her number and instructions to call anytime, day or night.

"Come on, let's go see your grandma," Michelle offered, walking her out under her arm.

"OK," Megan said since she had no choice. Soon they were back in the cop's car headed across the bridge to the Bronx.

****

"Go on up to Dianne's. I'll be up in a minute," Michelle said seeing Lil Wop in the courtyard. She was too distraught and sober to worry about anyone seeing her cop. Reese would no doubt see, but it didn't matter since she was headed to her apartment anyway.

"OK," Megan agreed, again because she had no choice. Her mother turned and marched through the court yard. Megan took a deep breath and sprinted in the building and up the flight of steps. She knocked on the door at the same time as her mother reached the dealers.

"Hey, baby! Where's your mother?" Dianne asked peering down the hallway for her daughter.

"She went to see her friend," she assumed correctly since that's where she usually went when they visited. She crossed the room and hopped on the perch in the window to see what she could see. The projects bustled with activity but she first watched her mom talk to the dealers on the bench.

"Sup yo. Let me holla at you inside," Michelle said when she reached Wop and company. He took a long pull of the blunt in his hand before passing it off and standing.

"Don't smoke all that shit," he advised with smoke billowing from his lips and nostrils. He followed behind Michelle watching her swaying hips under the short skirt. Michelle could feel Reese's eyes on her but not her daughter's as they stepped inside the building. At least her friend wouldn't know how much she copped so she could cuff some to take home.

"I need an ounce, and some weed," she said passing him a thousand dollars. She paid nine hundred for the coke and the extra hundred got her an ounce of weed to go with it. He charged her a little extra since he knew she had it.

"Yo, I only got like..." Lil Wop paused to take stock of his stock. He pulled several packs of several drugs from multiple pockets. "Like a seven of soft, and weed."

"Well, what's that?" she insisted of a larger packet of drugs. Two eight balls of powder wouldn't last no time with the way she was running through dope.

"Hard," he replied since it's the opposite of soft. The difference between soft coke and cooked crack is like a sling shot verses a bazooka.

"Let me get it," they both heard her say. She had an excuse to smoke and took it. He happily sold it to her since he knew what it meant. For one, she would be back a lot more often and spending a lot more money. Two, no one can maintain a drug habit long which meant he would soon get to fuck her fine ass. He would fuck her for as long as she remained fine because that too would just be a matter of time.

They made the transaction and he peeped under her skirt as she bounded up the stairs by twos. He caught a glimpse of ass cheeks before she was out of sight.

"Gonna smash that!" he vowed to himself and squeezed his dick. The blunt in rotation came back to mind so he rushed back outside and got in where he fit in.

"Damn, bitch!" Michelle chuckled when Reese snatched her door open as soon as she stepped out of the stairwell. The greedy look on her face would have scared her if she wasn't wearing one of her own.

"Sup, mama. I ain't know you was out this way!" Reese lied. She too kept watch on the courtyard so she wouldn't miss a thing.

"Yeah, I had to come talk to the cops about Rohan," she said deciding to keep the rest to herself. "Anyway, I got us an eight ball."

"That's it?" Reese reeled ungratefully. She knew full well the woman was spending real good with Wop. Knew first hand since the teen bragged about it all the time.

"Yeah, that's all he had. That and some hard, but I don't fuck with that," she said making eye contact like it was true.

"You ain't get none?" Reese whined. "We could have rolled up some woolie."

Michelle felt her stomach churn at the mention of the crack laced blunts they used to smoke. Luckily, Rohan had plucked her from the projects before it got too bad. He was gone now and that was too bad.

"Nah, but we got this," she said, minus eye contact. She dumped some of the three and a half grams on the table and began to chop and make lines.

"This me!" Reese announced and leaned in to inhale the thickest lines. Michelle stifled a snicker as her friend hogged what she set out. She indulged in a few lines over music, beer and a blunt. Her mind was too troubled to really enjoy the latest gossip. She was pregnant by the man who killed her husband and had half an ounce of crack in her purse. The latter actually worried her more than the first.

****

"Come on and eat nosey," Dianne called from the kitchen. The first summons didn't yield a grandchild so she came around the cinder block wall. "Girl, get out that window and come eat."

"I'm not..." Megan began until a hunger pain rang from below. It was only then that she realized that night fall had fallen over the projects. The young project dwellers had been replaced by slightly older ones. She backed out of the window after one more scan to make sure she didn't miss anything.

"I can make this!" she cheered seeing fried chicken and scalloped potatoes adorn the old school plate. "My mom taught me!"

"And who you think taught her!" the woman replied proudly. She knew she hadn't been the best mother but her recipe passed down a generation proved she wasn't the worse. She and her beloved grandchild had a pleasant conversation over dinner.

"Hey, Ma!" Michelle called out as she used her keys to enter. Guilt prevented her from making eye contact, but Dianne knew the cocaine jitters all too well from her decade on the dope. Time out her life she could never get back. She'd vowed never to go back down that road again. She would though to prevent her daughter and her daughter's daughter from going through what lay ahead for them if she didn't veer off the path she was on.

"Hey, baby," Dianne greeted and stood to hug her child. "Are you OK? Megan told me about the police."

"Megan need to mind her own fat ass business!" she barked while staring down at the girl. She assumed she'd told about her and Jax and the embarrassment turned to anger.

"No, baby. The police need to let you grieve and stop questioning you," the woman said letting her know that was all she knew.

"Oh, OK. Yeah, they say they got a suspect. I don't know him though," she lied looking at Megan. The smart girl nodded in agreement and solidarity. "Let me call us a car service to go home. Here."

"Thank you, baby," Dianne sang for the contribution to her Colt 45 fund. Technically, recovering addicts shouldn't drink either but malt liquor is light years away from crack. A distinction Michelle was about to find out for herself.

An hour and a half later Michelle woke her daughter as the driver pulled into their drive way. The sleeping girl pouted as she looked around. She nodded at her house and stepped from the vehicle as her mother confirmed the credit card payment.

"Should make that damn lady cop pay me back!" she grumbled of the two-hundred-dollar fare. Despite being offered a return ride out to the Island. The driver waited until she opened the door before pulling away. It was the short skirt, not chivalry that kept him. "Go to bed."

"OK, Mommy," Megan replied to the unnecessary order since she was full and sleepy.

Michelle drug along as she prepared to retire for her room. Perhaps she saw the invisible line she was crossing and was hesitant about crossing it. She checked to make see if the kitchen was clean, hoping she would have something to fuss about, but Megan had followed her instructions to the letter.

With nothing else to keep her she grabbed a beer from the fridge and headed to her room. She made sure her door was closed and retrieved the dope from her purse.

"Oh boy," she groaned as she crushed a small amount of the large amount of crack. She shrugged in response to the whisper to add a little more and did. It went on top of a line of green weed in a white rolling paper. A lick and a twist sealed it and it was takeoff time.

The drugs crackled in the silent room when she put a flame to the end of the joint and took a long pull. Her eyes went wide as the strong drug coursed through her system. It attached itself to everything it touched leaving its mark like a dog pissing on trees.

"Mmm," Michelle moaned in reply to the sudden and intense high. It felt so good she couldn't figure out how it could be wrong.

Now she was horny and high yet alone and lonely. She reached for the battery powered relief she kept in her night stand. A flip of the switch brought it to life with a gentle buzz. She placed it against her throbbing wetness and set a record for quickest orgasm in her life.

"Shit!" she shouted as she shivered and shook from coming real hard. As good as the vibrator felt it wasn't fucking with Jax, neither was she now that she knew he was involved in her husband's death. That still didn't stop her from calling him. "Come through whenever you finish doing whatever you doing. I'm horny!"

Chapter 23

"Yeah, yeah, oh yeah!" Jax exclaimed as he bust a nut on Zina from Zimbabwe flat stomach. With both Snake and XL out of the picture he had the run of club Back Shots and the race was on to bed every broad in the building. Snake's men could continue to run the place as long as he had the run of the place. This would speed up his mission to fuck every girl from every country. He kept a vigil for the sexy young girl Snake had but she didn't show up.

He and Junior decided to hang out and enjoy free drinks and pussy while talking business. Junior had Ilsa from Iceland bent over the arm of the sofa delivering back shots and wasn't far behind.

"Damn it, man!" he grunted and filled his condom. "You shoulda took this spot over a long time ago!"

"Well, it's ours now." Jax replied since late is still better than never. Now that pleasure was out the way they ran the girls off so they could talk business. "So, how do we handle your dad?"

"I'm not killing my father." Junior shot back shaking his head. He wanted and needed the old man out of the way but that was going too far. He crossed his heart for entertaining the thought of wacking his dad. Not that he hadn't thought of it, on many occasions, but he couldn't go through with it.

"We don't have to. Why not put him in a nice comfortable facility where he can eat good food. Play games, shuffleboard and shit," Jax suggested quite reasonably.

"You mean, like a nursing home?" he wondered and nodded at the idea. It was certainly more humane than what Snake had gotten.

"Well, I was thinking more like a federal penitentiary. I can hook him up," Jax said, playing his ace in the whole. He paused to sip his drink and let Junior chew on the unorthodox idea. "I got an inside track on all narcotics investigations in the tristate area. I know when the cops move before they do. I can make a case that sticks and get him out of our way."

"This is a valuable asset! How can you pull a feat like this off?" Junior challenged. He had been chunking money at cops for years looking for a man on the inside.

"Cuz, I'm a cop." he said tossing his badge on the table in front of them. There was a sudden silence that muted the camaraderie, drinks and weed. The music from the front of the club thumped loudly through the door while the man churned the information in his mind like butter. Junior wore a confused frown as he processed this new information. His lips twisted into a sideways smile and his head began to nod.

"Well, you can't be a very good cop!" he finally spoke and cracked up. "I see how this could work. We have an inside track on everything! You can bust our competition and we'll have the city on lock!"

"Exactly! See, I'm not an undercover cop playing drug dealer. I'm an undercover drug dealer playing cop. I'm a bad cop. The fucking worse!" Jax laughed. The two men began to laugh and drink once again. They ordered a couple more girls and went for round two as the partnership was consummated.

****

"Shit, I gotta get home. My girl is going to lose her mind," Junior said, shaking his head at the diamond hands on his diamond encrusted watch. He was pissy drunk and absolutely spent from sampling several vaginas from around the globe. The music cut out front signaling the club was closing.

"Damn!" Jax said checking his own watch. It was almost five proving time flies when you're having fun. The naked strippers laying around was proof of just how much fun was had.

The two young dealers were set to take over the New York drug market. That would mean Jersey and Connecticut was next. Philly, DC and the rest of the east coast was sure to follow. Unlike his father, Junior had no desire to go slow, move cautious. He wanted it all now which is the pride before the fall.

"See you this afternoon and we'll put that thing in motion," Junior said, raising his hand for a parting pound. That *thing* of course was setting his father up for a bust. Ten or twenty of the free kilos they had should do the trick.

"Um..." Jax said, stalling on the man hug and pointing down with his head.

"Oh, my bad." Junior laughed and put his dick away. A fist bump was now all that was appropriate so they bumped fist and separated.

211

Jax pulled out his phone as he stepped over the strippers scattered on the floor like litter. It buzzed a full minute from text and voicemails. He shook his head knowing his baby's mother had blew him up. This was going to cost him a shopping spree and he knew it. He shrugged at the idea since he was about to become very wealthy.

"Huh?" Jax asked as he listened to a message from Michelle as he stepped from their club. Her speech was garbled from the coke twisting her mouth like Bobby Brown but the words still didn't make sense.

He listened again to her rambles that went from horny to angry then something about a baby, then her husband and back to being horny again. His confusion didn't stop him from registering the sudden movement in the parking lot as he made his way to his car. He almost made a move for his gun but realized they had the drop on him so he tried his smile instead.

"Police! Freeze! Show me your hands!" came the shouts from all directions. Jax complied and raised his hands in surrender.

An officer dressed in SWAT attire rushed forward and snatched his hands from the air. He pulled them behind his back and secured them in cuffs. It was only then that the Captain stepped from a vehicle and came near.

"Sup, fellas? What's going on? Good morning, Captain." he greeted genially.

"Marcus Jackson, you're under arrest for the murder of Detective Rohan Robinson," he announced formally, then turned to the SWAT officer. "Take him away!"

****

"Well, well, well. Look who it is," Officer Davis jeered when Jax was brought into the precinct. She wasn't due in to work for a couple of hours but had come in early when news of the arrest spread. She and half of the first shift were present to see his perp walk of shame. The other half were tying up their own loose ends so they wouldn't be next.

"Sup, sexy" he replied, blowing her and winking his eye. He watched her large ass shift as she stormed off.

"In here," a SWAT officer directed as he steered Jax into an interrogation room. He cracked a smile at the thought of one of his peers attempting to get him to incriminate himself. Jax was a beast on one side of the interrogation table, but today he was seated on the opposite side.

"Thanks, buddy," Jax said incongruously at being cuffed to the table. He tried to remind the cop that they were once cool. Even though they attended the academy together he wouldn't look in his face. He shook his head as he left the room, locking the door behind him.

"Let him stew?" Pascal suggested since it was standard practice. Not today though because Marinetti couldn't wait to get at him.

"You stew!" he said and barged in on the cop turned murder suspect. Pascal stalled in place for a moment trying to decide what to do. A moment later he got up and followed his partner into the room.

"Sup, Johnny? I..." Jax greeted when the veteran detective walked in the room. He wasn't sure if his winning smile would help him but flashed it anyway just in case. It got cut short when Marinetti cut his greeting short.

"That's Detective Marinetti, you piece if shit cop killer," he barked, ready to bite. He unconsciously glanced up to the camera to remind him these weren't the good old days. The days where he would have use a telephone book to slap that smile off his face. Then use it to beat a confession out of him.

"Bruh, you got some proof I killed a cop? Humor me until my lawyer gets here," he dared even though he hadn't called one.

"OK, smart ass. Who's this?" Marinetti dared and played a clip of the recording.

"No. What I'm going to do is arrest him and XL for the murder of my sister. I'm going to arrest you too for obstruction if you get in my way."

"I'on know?" Jax said even though his furrowed brows spelled worried. The vet knew to be quiet and listen to find out just what they did know.

"You don't know huh?" Marinetti said with a humorless chuckle and played the next clip from the recording.

"Setting up an alibi. I respect the whole 'good cop' thing but I'm not one. I'm a bad cop. A black cop just like the song says."

"Guess, I'll call my lawyer." Jax said once he heard the murder on the recording. Luckily for him he had a couple of tricks left up his sleeve.

****

214

"Que pasa?" Ruiz demanded when the Maybach slowed and began to pull over. He was on his way to City Island for lunch and didn't like waiting.

"Policia!" the driver pleaded hoping the excuse would suffice the hard to please man. The old man was becoming more like an old lady every day.

"Por que?" he demanded, wanting to know why he was being pulled over. The driver shrugged since he had no idea. He wasn't speeding or changing lanes so he didn't have a clue.

Ruiz rolled his own window down to confront the cops before they even reached the driver. He was actually glad his hot-headed son, Junior, had begged off at the last minute because he would have made it worse. Not that he planned to go easy on them himself. He got even more irritated when the cop just sat in his car so he opened his door.

"Back in your vehicle!" The driver ordered through the intercom. He had to repeat the command once more before the stubborn old man complied.

Ruiz blamed his driver and berated him for the next fifteen minutes while they waited. The wait was over when an unmarked, all black suburban pulled up. It may have been unmarked but still had federal agents written all over it.

"Here we go again," Ruiz chuckled to himself when two and a half agents stepped out of the SUV. The half an agent let out a bark and wagged her tail eagerly.

"Is that right, girl?" the dog handler asked. He spoke dog and knew exactly what she was saying. It was K-9 for I can smell that shit from here! After a brief consultation with the beat car and the trio walked over to the car.

"Mr. Ruiz, can I get you and your driver to step from the car?" the agent asked. It sounded like question but was actually a command. The veteran drug lord knew the drill and quickly complied. The quicker he did the quicker he could go eat cracked crabs and lobsters.

"Make it quick! I'm on my way to City Island for lunch. Lobster as big as your head," he quipped in his usual pomp and arrogance.

"Yeah, well..." the agent nodded. The tip was almost too good to be true, but if it was true that would be too good.

The dog lost her little dog mind as she drew near the back seat. The handler lifted the seat forward and did a double take at the neat bricks of cocaine stacked under it. He smiled broadly and told his partner, "Look it!"

"Oh my! Mr. Ruiz, whose vehicle is this?" he asked formally.

"Mine! And everything in it is mine. I worked hard for it!" his shot back lifting his chin proudly. The drug enforcement agent proudly placed him in cuffs and recited his favorite tune.

"You have the right to remain silent..."

****

"You believe him?" Pascal asked as they followed up on the lead provided by Jax through his attorney.

"I don't believe anything that cock sucker has to say!" Marinetti barked as they approached the residence. The smell of death emanated through the door before they could open it.

216

The warrant was of the *no knock* variety so they didn't knock. Instead a burly cop used a battering ram to knock it off its hinges.

"Police! Search warrant!" he screamed even though it was evident from the smell that whoever was here couldn't hear. Death has the tendency to make one deaf as well. The cops fanned out to clear the house room by room.

"Detectives!" one called from the bed room. The homicide detectives followed their ears and nose to the room.

"Snake I presume." Marinetti said shaking his head at Snake laid out with a hole in his head. He had no clue who the dead girl beside him was or what she had to do with him.

"Look," Pascal said pointing to the open safe. It was almost empty except for a brand-new Glock pistol.

"Bet you dollars to doughnuts this was the weapon that killed Robinson," Marinetti said twisting his lips dubiously. This was too simple, too pat to be true. His head shook once more now that it was clear Jax had just beat a murder charge. Giving up Ruiz and Snake wasn't quite a *get out of jail free card*, but it saved him from the lethal injection. Now all they had on him was the drugs found in his condo. It would cost a couple of decades of his life but spared it.

Junior vowed to keep him in the loop and on payroll until he returned in return for getting his dad out of his way. This was the end but the story is far from over.

Epilogue

I've had plenty of bad days in my young life, but I'll always remember this as one of the worse. The smug look on Jax's face when he was sentenced will always haunt me. I would have felt better if he was some hideous, three-headed monster but instead he was a gorgeous man with a beautiful smile. A smile made wider when the murder charges were dropped in exchange for giving up Ruiz on trumped up charges fabricated by Jax and his own son. Jax was still going to prison but would be rich when he got out. Fifteen years seemed like a lot time, but it's not. Before I know it, I'll have to deal with him coming home. I'll be a cop by then which means he'll have to deal with me as well.

Please enjoy the following excerpt of Lies &
Manipulation, A Southern Love Story by Sa'id
Salaam

Chapter 1

"Girl, let me see what he working with!" Shandera fussed
as she took Bella's phone out of her hand. The animated
woman was always fussing whether she was happy or sad,
melancholy or mad. Part of her theatrics were a frown,
grimace or twisted lip at whatever was going on at the
moment.

At this moment, they were discussing Bella's latest suitor;
well, his dick, anyway. There were plenty of conversations at
Bella's beauty salon but most had something to do with
somebody's dick. Even a conversation about the pastor's latest
sermon would somehow get a dick in it. Food, dick. The
weather, dick. Music, dick. Dick, dick, dick the long day
through.

"Damn, girl!" Bella complained about her snatching her
phone away. She may have been the boss but most times, she
was one of the girls. She put a hand on her shapely hip and
batted her greyish eyes in mock protest. Technically, her
French, Indian and African American mix made the girl a
mutt, but it came together to form an exotic beauty that turned

heads everywhere she went. She couldn't keep a man, though, which explained the new dick pic in her phone.

"I know that's right! I needs to see the dick up front!" Alexis huffed. The big woman was fronting, though, because she couldn't take any dick anyway. The average six-inch variety would have her whooping and hollering like an Indian on the warpath.

"It's the little dicks you gotta look out for! All four of my baby daddies got little dicks," a customer added from Shandera's chair.

The hairdresser stayed in hot demand due to her skills and vibrant personality. She was a name brand to be dropped, like Prada or Gucci. She only played second fiddle to Bella, who was widely regarded as the best hairdresser in the city, if not state, East of the mighty Mississippi, have her tell it. There was a rivalry right beneath the epidermis of their friendship but it was to be expected since every Jesus needs a Judas. It's the cost one paid to be the boss. And being the boss meant you just had to stay on guard for the inevitable cross.

"Eh, it's okay. No bumps or bruises. Nice curve, good veins," Shandera said as she analyzed the prospective penis. She turned and twisted the phone to view the dick from different angles. The woman was an expert after all when it came to dicks. A dick-ologist, if you will. "Seven, maybe eight inches. If he know how to work it, you may be in business."

"Chile, let me see this thang!" Sherbert, the resident sissy, hissed like sissies do. He then rubbed his big hands on his apron and came over to inspect. "Mm-hm...un-huh...I know him! Dennis McDaniels, age 32, lives at 25 Lafayette Court in the 7th Ward."

All mouths gaped at the news, except for Bella, that is. She just shook her head and laughed. The girls often sicced the sissy on any guy they thought about getting serious with. A sad fact was that a lot of the men out there would fuck with a man if they could get away with it. Only the owner of this particular penis wasn't named Dennis and he wasn't from 7th Ward.

"Eeehh! Wrong answer!" Bella buzzed like a game show. "That ain't him and he ain't from here!"

That was all they were getting out of her about her long-distance lover. They were still cultivating each other after meeting on social media a few months ago. The subject finally got around to sex, hence the dick pic. Most dudes will shoot one off in a second to a woman's inbox. Not Gavin. No; he took it slow.

"But, how you know that's really his? Dudes catfish dicks, you know," Alexis threw in, and she was right. Some will catfish a whole body and photoshop their head on it. Yes, it's deceptive, but so are contacts and lace fronts. Those may not be his pecs or abs, but some women don't look nothing like their pictures, either. Many a man have taken a woman home only to wake up to another one."

"Girl, what kind of man would have pictures of another man's penis in his phone?" Bella demanded to know in a WTF tone.

"Um...right here, Chile!" Sherbert raised a hand and waved.

The whole shop cracked up and cackled in laughter. No matter how miserable life could be on the outside, the shop was always good for a laugh. There were plenty of tears as well.

"My point exactly," Bella cosigned.

"Oh yeah, Sherbert, what's up with ole boy I asked you about?" Baby Girl asked hopefully. The nineteen-year-old had just completed cosmetology school and landed her job at the hottest salon in New Orleans. The job was part luck, part charity since Bella knew her mother from around The Ward. Her story was similar to her own, so she had to show love.

Angelique's mother, Demetria, had her at fourteen, by sixteen she was using dope, and was dead by seventeen, leaving her baby girl behind. The whole hood adopted the baby and dubbed her Baby Girl. The hood stood up and got her through high school and then cosmetology school. Baby Girl had a penchant for the bad boys she grew up around. Luckily for her, she had Sherbert and the rest of the gang to school her on them.

"Who, Slugga? He gay!" he nodded in agreement as he whipped out his phone with the proof. They always wanted proof when it was a dude they really liked. Even though sometimes that didn't stop some if they really, really liked a guy. It was one of the reasons the HIV rate was so high in the city. Another was the constant tourism that helped diseases flow to and fro, far and wide. People came for Mardi Gras and left with a lot more than beads. In the city's defense, plenty of those tourists arrived with diseases of their own, trading STDs like baseball cards.

"Damn shame!" Baby girl fumed, seeing the goon with dreads and gold teeth butt-naked in the sissy's phone. His jailhouse fine frame was covered in crude tats, adding to his ghetto appeal. He was gay, though, so, "You can have him."

"I already did! You can get him back," Sherbert laughed twice, once at his little joke and again at the look of utter disgust on the young girl's face. It was exactly the reaction she should have had.

She made a big production out of deleting his number from her phone and him from her life. Bella nodded her head in approval, as it was the reaction she expected. She couldn't watch the girl forever. She may own the hottest salon in the city, but she was making plans to leave.

"Girl, how you end up with a building in the French Quarter anyway?" a newer patron asked, knowing that the buildings in the gentrified city were worth millions and Bella was barely thirty.

"Oh boy!" Shandera groaned playfully even though she was serious. She had heard the story about Bella's grandmother a hundred times already. This would make a hundred and one as Bella fondly recalled the come up of the woman who raised her.

Chapter 2

"My Grandma was a bad bitch back before bitches was supposed to be bad. A hustler fo' real…"

"Monsieur Beufonte, the new cook is here," the maid announced with a timbre of fear in her voice. She should be scared, after what happened with the last cook. The one who got chased out of the estate with a butcher knife in her back and her panties at her ankles.

"Let me see her!" Mrs. Beufonte insisted, rushing ahead of her husband since he was the problem. She'd walked in on her husband and the last cook having oral sex in the pantry. She'd specifically requested a black woman this time, hoping that would keep his dick out of her. Her racist French husband certainly wouldn't stoop that low, or so she thought.

Mr. Beufonte followed behind her stoically. Business was good here in New Orleans but what he loved most about America was the loose women. All of his rich aristocrat friends regularly had sex with the help. While France was known as the country of romance, they were fucking over here in the United States. He had no use for the black servants most of the city's elite families used but loved all the white trash the Deep South had to offer.

With a name like Bella, both the Beufontes were expecting a big black woman in a white dress with a rag wrapped around her head. They thought they'd have to train her in the fine art of French cooking, just like the last one. Both were shocked, however, when they actually saw Bella. She was black, alright, but the only thing fat on her was concealed in her panties. The tight white dress snitched on the roundness of her ass and flatness of her chest.

"Perfect!" Mrs. Beufonte cheered and cracked up at the woman, knowing her husband wouldn't touch her. She was so busy laughing at her black skin that she missed how smooth it was. Nor did she catch how it contrasted with her dark grey eyes that produced a seductive look about her. However, what she did notice was her thick black hair. It was done in big bouncy curls that shined in the Louisiana sun.

"Gal, who did that to your hair?" Mrs. Beufonte demanded, as if she had done something wrong.

"Never mind her hair. Can she cook French food?" Mr. wanted to know. "I do not eat this, this garbage they eat over here!"

"Funny, because didn't I walk in on you eating garbage in the pantry?" she shot back. The help ducked their heads to conceal their mirth.

That was enough to send him rushing red-faced from the room. All eyes shot to Bella who lifted her head like a person who liked attention.

"Well, to answer yo' questions, I shole can cook French food. My mama cooked for a French family for thirty-years. Twenty with me right by her side and taught me everything she knowed," she replied proudly.

Her mother had cooked and cleaned herself to death for other people, dying without a dime. Bella vowed she'd never live or die like her mother. She socked away every extra coin she earned to one day have her own. Her own beauty salon, that is, because cooking was just a means to an end.

"And, your hair?" Mrs. asked once more. She fully intended to hire whoever did the black girl's hair. If someone could turn nappy black hair into bouncy curls then they would work wonders with her luscious blonde locks.

"I did it myself," Bella replied, lifting her chin even higher in pride. "I'm also a beautician!"

"More like a magician than beautician. You turned nappy copper into smooth silk," the woman of the house said, offending Bella for a second time. Bella had a three strike rule like in baseball, except she would fuck your man upon the third infraction.

"My mama was Indian!" she huffed indignantly in explanation of her sinuous hair, a battle she'd fought her whole life in her native 7th Ward.

"Did she put a spell on your nappy hair to make it like that?" she asked for strike three. "Can you do my hair?"

"I'm here to cook! Now, if you want to hire me on my off time, that'll be just fine."

"Fine," Mrs. Beufonte huffed in agreement. "I'll give you five whole dollars to do my hair, if you make it look just like yours."

"No, you won't. I charges ten, whole, dollars to do hair," Bella insisted. She knew her worth in the kitchen, bedroom and salon. Some days she would work all three, only to sock all the money away. Rent for her half of the duplex shotgun *house wasn't much so the rest got saved to purchase her dream.*

"Fine, ten dollars then!" Mrs. huffed, like she had a choice. She didn't because, again, Bella knew her worth.

Bella did the woman's hair and she was soon the envy of all the socialites. She paid top dollar to stunt on her friends. Her worth was about to go up...

****

"Police chasing Slugga dem through the square!" Hustle-Man announced as he walked in. The booster, import/export, wholesale retailer always had the latest everything in everyone's sizes.

"Oh no!" Baby girl fussed and ran to the window just as Slugga blew past in a stolen Volvo. He was blowing a blunt of loud and laughing even louder as he ran from the police.

"Didn't he just say that boy was gay?" Shandera demanded, scrunching up her pretty face.

"Chile, they don't care. You know how many gals I gotta fight 'bout they man!" Sherbert said, shaking his head.

"Anyway, what you got for us today?" Bella turned to Hustle-Man and asked. She had plenty of money but wasn't above saving some cool cash buying the hot goods.

"What don't I got?" he shot back. The tall, handsome man was the perfect salesman. He could work at any of the city's elite dealerships and get rich, but he was addicted to the streets and the city's drug of choice; heroin. He was a functioning junkie who kept up his appearance. There was another junkie just like him who worked in the salon. One of its beautiful beauticians was also a junkie.

The women, along with Sherbert, gathered around and perused the merchandise. Hustle-Man sold Fire Sticks, DVDs of the latest Hollywood movies and porn, shirts, shoes, watches and maxi pads. By the time he left, his bag was empty and his pockets were full. Time to see the dope man.

"I'm gonna wear these on my date tonight," Bella announced, holding a pair of earrings up to her ears.

"Thought you had a long-distance boo?" Shandera pried like she always did. For some reason, she needed an explanation for everything everyone did.

"I do, *but he long-distance,*" she laughed. "A bitch still gotta eat!"

Chapter 3

Bella couldn't help but feel a wave of pride whenever she pulled up to her house. The old shotgun house had come a long way since her grandmother bought it decades ago; even Katrina tried and couldn't destroy it. She'd totally renovated the damaged duplex and transformed it into a single-family home. It was the nicest house on the block, if not in the whole 7th Ward. She got plenty of offers for it, just like she did for her third share of the French Quarter building that housed the salon, but neither was for sale. Not just yet, anyway.

Her laptop dinged to alert her of a new message. Unlike most of her employees and clients, she did her social media in private. Most of the women in the shop stayed glued to their screens. However, none of her employees or clients were allowed in that part of her world. Now she could be whoever she wanted to be and no one could say otherwise.

Welcome home. How was your day? Gavin asked via private message.

You watching me or something? How you know I just walked in? she shot back quickly. She hadn't bothered to kick off her heels or sit her purse down before jumping online to boo love with her new love interest.

You come home the same time every day, duh.

Oh yeah, lol, she said and genuinely laughed. It was true, too. She made it her business to get straight home to inbox with him. They had exchanged phone numbers to talk and text, but still inboxed each other since that's how it started.

So, what you think? he asked, cocking his head cockily as he asked about the picture of his cock.

'Bout what? she asked coyly and giggled. She liked the dick pic just fine, so did the girls at the shop. Oh, and Sherbert, too.

Yeah right. Hope you ain't been showing my man around the beauty parlor.

Me? No! I would never! she typed and laughed out loud in real life.

Hey, gotta go... he typed urgently and was gone.

Bella was used to it by now so shrugged her shoulders as she logged off to go and get ready for her dinner date.

"Who was that? I hope we ain't about to go through this again, Gavin Mitchell!" Mrs. Mitchell fussed. Her handsome husband was quite the internet sensation, even if he wasn't talking about much in real life. It's hard to be an international playboy with a wife and four kids.

****

Bella was so fine even she liked looking at herself naked. She enjoyed the striptease in the full-length mirror as she removed her work clothes. She turned sideways to check out her booty then turned straight again to marvel at her flat stomach. She flung her lovely locks back and then did a little shimmy and giggled. Once she was satisfied that she was a certified bad bitch, she peeled off her panties and bra and stepped into the shower.

"Guuuurl," Bella warned when a shiver ran through her body as she washed between her legs. It was a reminder of how long it had been since she'd had sex.

Ten years back, Bella went through a hoe phase in her life. Not that she'd slept with a whole lot of men, but most of the men she had slept with was during that time. She'd been in college and there was a lot of fucking going on. During that time, Darren Thibodeux was one of the men who'd laid claim to that sweet juice box between her thighs. He'd spent the last ten years since then trying to get back inside. That, and making millions of legal and illicit dollars.

"Hmp!" Bella fussed at the thought of letting Darren hit it again.

He could've been the one, if he hadn't had sex with Shandera. He wasn't Bella's man, so she couldn't be mad at either one of them. Shandera often fucked behind her, like the person with the little shovel who walks behind a horse. He'd never be her man but as long as Darren wanted to feed her and throw gifts at her, she would accept them. He just wasn't getting any pussy.

Bella had converted one of the spare bedrooms into a closet during the post-Katrina renovation. It was more like an upscale boutique than a closet. She could literally spend hours inside playing dress up, just like she did when she'd played in Grandma Bella's clothes way back when. Her collection of designer shoes, dresses and handbags were worth more than the houses on both sides of her, combined.

However, there wasn't time to play tonight since Darren had reservations at one of the most exclusive restaurants in The Quarter. Foolishly, he assumed it would do the trick to get back inside of her. It wouldn't; she just wanted to try their crawfish étouffée that was supposed to be all that.

"Hmp!" she huffed again at the notion of someone making a better étouffée than Grandma Bella. Her grandmother had been a cross between Superman and Wonder Woman in her eyes. She was the epitome of the best of everything. "Hmp!" she huffed a final time upon hearing the distinct honk of the Lamborghini out front. "Wish I would go running out like some thot!"

"Oh yeah," Darren laughed out loud at himself. He knew Bella was nothing like the thots he fed his dick to on a daily basis. She had her own bread and she wasn't impressed with his. He'd worked hard to reach this station in life, so he knew hard work paid off. Bella was the one, so he had no problem working to get her. He planned to wife her up, by any means necessary.

Chapter 4

[Double Click To Add Text]

CPSIA information can be obtained
at www.ICGtesting.com
Printed in the USA
LVOW10s1819180917
549133LV00014B/979/P